BAD MAN'S RANGE

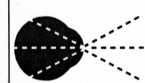

This Large Print Book carries the
Seal of Approval of N.A.V.H.

BAD MAN'S RANGE

JACKSON COLE

WHEELER PUBLISHING
A part of Gale, Cengage Learning

GALE
CENGAGE Learning·

Detroit • New York • San Francisco • New Haven, Conn • Waterville, Maine • London

GALE
CENGAGE Learning®

LIBRARY OF CONGRESS CATALOGING-IN-PUBLICATION DATA

Cole, Jackson.
  Bad Man's Range / by Jackson Cole. — Large Print edition.
    pages cm. — (Wheeler Publishing Large Print Western)
  ISBN 978-1-4104-6151-3 (softcover) — ISBN 1-4104-6151-3 (softcover)
  1. Large type books. I. Title.
PS3505.O2685B33 2013
813'.54—dc23   2013017323

Published in 2013 by arrangement with Golden West Literary Agency

Printed in the United States of America
-1 0 1 2 3   17 16 15 14 13

CHAPTER I
KEEP OFF!

The river, which ran north to south where Mullen City squatted on its east bank, caught the pale glow of the moon. An occasional oil light showed in a window, but for the most part the town slept for the day to come. And though it was after midnight, the earth still retained much of the warmth beaten into it by the south Texas sun.

A square frame house stood in its yard on the north side of town. A few bushes and dispirited scrub trees grew in sandy soil around it. The house was dark and the men in the back yard had left their horses behind the stable and crept close.

"Yuh shore Davis sleeps alone in the corner room?" one said in a whisper. He looked large in the gloom.

"Shore as I savvy this is Davis's home, chief!"

"I don't want any mistakes," said the big man.

7

There were half a dozen others, all armed. Most of them wore Stetsons and riding clothes common to the range.

At the leader's signal two men came up with a ladder they had brought from the barn, and set it against the house wall. It reached an open second-story window and a bony fellow went up with a monkey's quiet agility.

The rest waited, hearing only a few muffled sounds from the upstairs bedroom. Then the scrawny fellow stuck his head out the window, saying softly:

"I got him!"

"Go up and give him a hand," commanded the chief, with a wave at a man nearby.

The man designated climbed the rungs and the others took down the ladder and went around back. Soon a bolt was drawn at the kitchen door and the pair who had gone into the darkened house brought out a limp figure, a bandanna gag over the lips.

"Yuh fetch his clothes?" asked the leader.

They had, a bundle containing pants, shirt, boots, and a hat. They left the back door unlocked and went to their horses, held by another member of the crew in the ebony shadow cast by the barn.

"Leave the corral bars down," said the big

man, as a black horse in the pen was caught.

They fastened their victim to the bare back of the black.

"Now saddle up that other gelding," ordered the chief. "And let's go. We can't push our luck too far."

A rider went ahead to scout the way, but no one stirred about the settlement. There was no bridge across the river but there was a shallows to the north where they might cross easily. A ragged line of brush along the west bank made a convenient screen.

West and southwest the moon shone on an apparently endless range, rolling, grassy and broken only by hummocks and a few patches of woods and rocks. But northwest were black hills covered with stands of timber and with sharp rock spires thrusting to the sky.

They rode toward this distant objective for a time and then the big man pulled up by a clump of cottonwoods. "This is as good a place as any," he announced.

"He's wakin' up," said his bony aide.

The gagged victim was pulled from his horse and propped against a tree. His eyes rolled white in the moonlight and he moaned a bit. The large man and his helper drew Colts and without more ado fired into the helpless captive.

"Fray the lead rope on that black so it will look like he broke loose, and let him roam," snapped the boss. "Turn the saddled animal free. I'll see you boys later."

Death had struck in the peaceful Texas night. . . .

A sign in bold letters read sternly:

KEEP OFF!
YOU ARE ON MACE RANGE.
TRESPASSERS SEVERELY PUNISHED!
COL. MADISON CRILE

"Corky" Ellsworth glanced at the board nailed to a pine bole stuck in the earth. It was one of many such he had passed.

"This Mace outfit ain't what yuh'd call hospitable, Whitefoot," Ellsworth murmured to his horse.

But Ellsworth was not afraid of any man. He stood six feet in his half-boots and he could protect himself in the sort of ruckus a rider might run into in south Texas.

His strong body was clad in leather pants and a blue shirt with the sleeves rolled up. A leather vest hung open, and a red kerchief circled his lean throat. The chin strap of his Stetson was loose in its runner and crisp light hair curled around his generous ears. The lines at the corners of his blue eyes

10

showed how easily he laughed.

"The Mace owns a mighty big hunk of Texas," went on Ellsworth as Whitefoot flicked an appreciative ear. The cowboy was thinking how many warnings he had passed as he pushed south for Mullen City, and of the Mace brand. It was different from any he had ever seen before — a club design with knobs on a round head.

Corky Ellsworth had spent the last three years across the Pecos, but recently had bought a small ranch on the Edwards Plateau not far from San Antonio. He was on his way to see about purchasing breeder cattle from a dealer near Mullen.

He could tell good range when he saw it and he was looking at it now. On the north, foothills rode to wooden heights which shielded the rolling grazing lands from storms. Curling, nutritious grasses had come in thick where mesquite and other weedy growth had been cut. No wonder they were so anxious to keep people off it.

Ellsworth had made another mile when he heard something hum overhead. He turned quickly for he knew how a heavy rifle bullet sounded as it ripped through the atmosphere. He believed he had been sighted and was being further advised to get off the Mace.

A long spine of rock projecting south from the hills had cut off his view to the west but this diminished in the fashion of an alligator's tail until it was lost in the plain. The wind came from that direction and borne by it, Ellsworth heard cracking shots and the hoarse shouts of angry men. Then he saw half a dozen riders galloping around a wooded grove below the terminus of the ridge. They were pouring lead in at someone concealed in the copse.

Ellsworth at first had no notion of taking a hand in what did not concern him. He was on strange ground and did not know the rights and wrongs of the matter. For all he knew those attackers might be rooting out a rustler.

He saw then that not far from the grove was a dead mustang, and beyond this lay a man. A saddled horse was galloping off.

"Mighty tough on somebody," growled Ellsworth. "They shot one hombre and got the other holed up!"

He decided that the slug he had heard singing by his own head had been a stray and not intended for him at all, for the horsemen did not seem to be aware of him. But a moment later one spied him and pointed, yelling to the others. Three left the scrap around the grove and started for him, opening fire with carbines. Ellsworth again heard the whine of bullets.

He pulled Whitefoot's rein to ride off. This was none of his affair. But suddenly the unprovoked attack angered him and he jerked his rifle from its holster and pumped a cartridge into the breech. He didn't like the looks of those three men headed for him.

They kept shooting and plainly were trying to kill him. Ellsworth turned in his saddle and took aim at the man in the center. As soon as he pressed trigger he was sure he had made a hit. It was proved when the rider clapped a hand to his head and flew from his seat, landing hard and sliding several feet before he stopped.

The others slowed, but kept blasting at Ellsworth, though their bullets were wild. Ellsworth shifted his attention to the pursuer on the right. He must have made another good shot for the man jumped, whirled and headed back toward the grove. The third gave up then, and followed on the run.

Ellsworth was free to ride on now but by this time he was burning up with anger. Besides, the looks of those horsemen and the way they had fired on him for no reason told him they could scarcely be honest cowboys. He wondered whom they had trapped in the grove, and why.

He swung Whitefoot and trotted back to the man he had shot from saddle. The riders down below were still keeping an eye on him, but they also were still trying for their quarry in the trees. One caught a bullet through the shoulder and let the world know it by howling and clutching at his wound.

Ellsworth knew they were watching him as he coolly got down to examine the crumpled gunslinger. A ragged furrow showed in the greasy hair. Ellsworth had only creased the man whose face was bearded and sallow, and who gave all outward indication of being an unsavory character.

"Rustlers or worse," muttered Ellsworth, his jaw set. "Now what?"

He would have given aid to the man he had shot, except that the fellow's companions began throwing long shots his way. Plainly their intention was to drive him away, but he stood his ground with his carbine up and ready. They drew off and held a consultation. Presently they all came riding at Ellsworth, yelling and shooting.

Ellsworth squatted and got ready for them. The next bullet from his rifle slashed the leader of the party — and this was enough. The howling riders turned tail and fled, hurried on their way by the bang of Ellsworth's gun.

Picking up speed, they were going at full tilt when they reached the protection of the ridge and made for the rough country to the northwest.

Ellsworth quit firing and straightened up, staring after them. A broad grin spread across his face.

A loud hail came from the grove.

"Hey, there!"

Ellsworth turned his head to the copse.

"Who are yuh?" he called. "Come on out! The buskins have hightailed."

From the brush and rocks a burly figure emerged, walking with the rolling gait of a rider. He wore leather but had lost his hat in the fight. In one hand he carried a heavy rifle, and a cartridge belt supporting a Colt circled his waist. He was cautious as he came toward Ellsworth, who also was alert.

He pulled up a few yards away to eye Ellsworth and the bearded man on the ground who was beginning to twitch and grunt.

"I owe yuh thanks," said the heavy young fellow. Even in his stress Ellsworth noticed that his voice had a pleasing ring.

"They came at me first," replied Ellsworth grimly.

"Lucky for me they did. I was runnin' out of rifle ammunition. Sooner or later they'd have got me. I'm Jeff Crile."

"My handle is Ellsworth. I'm just ridin' through. You the owner of this range?"

"My old man is. I was up this way with one of our *vaqueros* when we were ambushed. Rafael — he was the *vaquero* — they got him. Almost got me, too, but I managed to make that grove after they shot my hoss."

Ellsworth studied Jeff Crile, the barrel chest and sturdy limbs, the good features and clear brown eyes. Crile had curly black hair and a strong jaw. He also was studying Corky Ellsworth. Suddenly his face broke into a smile and he came forward with a big hand extended. He had made up his mind. Also, there was a bond in the common peril they had just experienced. They gripped hands.

"What yuh say we tie up this cuss and run him to the ranch?" suggested Jeff Crile, nodding at the man on the ground.

"Yuh savvy who he is?" asked Ellsworth.

"One of the tough bunch who hide out in our hills," replied young Crile, with a scornful look at the wounded man.

"I saw yore signs," said Ellsworth apologetically. "I wouldn't have crossed yore range but I'm a stranger here and on my way to Mullen City. I kept tryin' to get clear of yore land but it's mighty wide."

Jeff Crile grinned. "I'll say again it was plumb lucky for me yuh showed." He grew serious as he went on. "We've had lots of trouble not only with outlaws but with other folks. The signs have been kind of necessary. Well — come on."

CHAPTER II
THE MACE

The Mace *vaquero's* mustang had stopped to graze down near the grove and Ellsworth roped the mount while Crile secured the prisoner. That accomplished, the two headed across the range together.

The ranch stood on a tributary of the river Ellsworth had been following. When they came in sight of the ranch-house he saw that it was of adobe bricks whitewashed and gleaming in the bright sunshine. He was impressed by the great *hacienda* with its many wings and patio in Spanish style. There were barns, stables and other structures.

There were cowboys in the yard. Half were lean Mexicans and the rest of Anglo-Saxon strain. They strolled forward curiously to see what Jeff and Ellsworth had brought in. Young Crile had the prisoner slung in front of him while Ellsworth had fetched in Rafael's body.

"What's up, Jeff?" sang out a waddy.

"Me and Rafael got ambushed and he caught one," replied Crile.

The captive was conscious now, and his muddy eyes rolled in fright as the Mace outfit surrounded him.

"This here cuss is one of the killers," went on Crile. His look was not reassuring as he glared at the gunslinger.

Jeff turned from the prisoner and his expression grew pleasant. "I want you boys to meet Corky Ellsworth. He saved my hide and he's a friend. Don't ever forget that."

All eyes briefed Ellsworth for a moment and he underwent a steady, silent attention with a slow grin.

An elderly man, an erect figure in gray trousers, wool shirt, and a cavalry Stetson came out of a side door.

"Jeff, my boy!" he called.

"I'm home, Dad!" answered Jeff, and his father came to them.

"This is Corky Ellsworth, Dad," Jeff said. "A passel of them bandits downed Rafael and shot my hoss from under me. Ellsworth routed 'em."

Colonel Madison Crile, owner of the Mace, was a man of fierce pride. He was a lean man who held himself with a military carriage, his chin up, his black eyes penetrating. He had fine silver hair and his goatee and mustache were of the same hue. Lines etched his face and he did not smile, although when he spoke to Ellsworth it was with the deepest courtesy.

"Welcome to the Mace, suh. What yuh done makes yuh one of us."

He turned to his son and his eyes darkened as he looked on the dead Rafael and the cringing captive while he heard young Crile's account of the fight.

The wealth and power of the Mace were obvious to Corky Ellsworth. The ranch had its own blacksmith shop, bakery and store and Corky knew it raised a large percentage of its food supply. Mexican women who lived on the place, wives of *vaqueros,* were skilled at making cloth and other articles. Their homes were a short distance from the *hacienda* in cabins built for married cowhands. Corky took a quick view of the outfit while Jeff told his father of the ambushing.

Then the prisoner was handed over to a couple of *vaqueros* to be locked up and guarded.

The excitement over, Ellsworth found that he was limping. He hadn't noticed it before, but he had pulled a muscle in his left leg during the fight. Also he was hungry, and needed rest. He was thankful that Colonel

Crile and Jeff seemed to take it for granted that he was going to remain at least overnight as the guest of the family.

His hosts escorted him to the massive front entry in the adobe wall. Through this he could see a large patio planted with flowers and shrubs and with chairs and tables placed about. There the family could enjoy the sun in complete privacy.

Two ladies sat there, drinking tea. One was middle-aged, the other with a budding flower's beauty. Ellsworth stopped short and pulled off his Stetson.

"Madre mia!" said Jeff Crile. He bent to kiss his mother's hand.

She had the proud look of the Castilian lady, and only one glance was needed to see that the girl had inherited her loveliness from her Spanish mother.

"Little sister Lucia!" Ellsworth heard Jeff saying.

Lucia was slim, and she wore a jeweled comb in her dark hair. Her expressive brown eyes looked with frank curiosity at their tall, light-haired guest. Ellsworth thought he caught the trace of a smile on her red lips.

The colonel brought Ellsworth forward as Jeff spoke in rapid Spanish to his mother. Mrs. Crile jumped up and threw her arms about her son, and from her fervor Ellsworth knew that Jeff had just told her how nearly he had been killed and that the visitor had saved his life.

The senora turned to Ellsworth, her eyes shining as she kissed him and thanked him. Jeff grinned and the colonel smiled indulgently. Evidently he was used to his wife's emotional displays.

"Sis, this is Corky Ellsworth," said Jeff. "Salt of the earth. He's stayin' with us."

"I'm happy to meet you, sir," said Lucia.

Ellsworth felt himself flushing as he murmured something to the girl. For Mrs. Crile kept hugging his arm and thanking him again and again for saving her boy. Ellsworth was uncomfortable. He was well aware that he needed a cleaning up, that he must appear rough to these ladies. And he was not certain — but was the lovely Lucia secretly laughing at him?

He was glad when Jeff took him to young Crile's own quarters. There he washed up and put on clean clothing which Jeff pressed on him.

"Yuh got a mighty fine outfit here, Jeff," he commented.

"*Si,* it's a fine ranch," agreed Crile. He spoke the colloquial language of the range interspersed with Spanish words and phrases. "It would be perfect if it wasn't for some hombres. The world's apt to be that way. It's mighty interestin' and yuh could have a real good time but there's always folks tryin' to spoil things."

"Yuh mean them outlaws?"

Jeff shrugged. "We wouldn't mind that so much. They're like vermin. Yuh have to clean 'em out now and then when they get too thick. The thing is — the world seems to be against the Mace."

"How so?"

Jeff turned aside the question. He went to pour a drink for Ellsworth.

Ellsworth ate dinner with the family, the great table presided over by Colonel Crile and his wife. The visitor was an honored guest. Lucia talked with him and in the evening she sang and played the guitar. This certainly was a magic spot, thought Corky Ellsworth.

He slept that night in a feather bed covered with silk, a strange contrast to the rough bunk of a cowboy. . . .

After breakfast next morning Jeff Crile said:

"We're ridin' to Mullen City, Ellsworth."

"I'll go along," Ellsworth said promptly. "That was where I was headin' anyway. I got business there."

Jeff hesitated, then shrugged. "Yuh're

welcome to travel with us," he said slowly. "But first yuh better find out whether yuh really want to or not."

"Shore I want to. Why shouldn't I?" Ellsworth couldn't understand, except that he scented mystery of some sort.

"We're runnin' that prisoner to the courthouse and we're goin' to charge him with killin' Rafael," Jeff said. "And I told yuh, that folks are against the Mace."

"I ain't, Jeff. I'm for yuh. What you say — and do — goes with me."

Jeff did not argue any more.

When Ellsworth went to saddle Whitefoot, twenty Mace riders were already waiting, heavily armed.

Colonel Crile came out and mounted a black gelding to lead his men. Then Lucia, in riding clothes, crossed the yard and came up to Ellsworth.

"We hope you come again and soon," she said softly. There was no hint of laughter in her manner now. And she added, "Please don't judge the Mace too harshly."

"I couldn't, ma'am," Corky assured her.

She stood there, waving to them, as the cavalcade got under way. . . .

That afternoon the Mace entered Mullen City. It was a large town on the east bank of the river, built around a square plaza with the courthouse and city hall on the commons. There were lines of stores, saloons and homes, and a Mexican quarter at the south end.

"Last chance to quit the Mace, Ellsworth," warned Jeff Crile, as they moved in.

But Ellsworth shook his head and rode with the watchful crew to the courthouse. Colonel Crile dismounted and went inside. After a time the Mace chief emerged and signaled the men to bring in the prisoner. A magistrate was just taking his seat as the cowboys shoved the gunslinger before him. "What's the charge?" demanded the judge.

"Killin', suh," replied Colonel Crile. "He and his gang shot down one of my boys on Mace range yesterday."

The magistrate frowned. "Got a lawyer?" he asked the captive.

"One moment, Judge! I represent this prisoner!"

A man came hurrying up the aisle, a commanding figure. He wore a blue suit and white stock set with a diamond flasher. His square face was adorned with a crisp brown mustache. Pomade kept his hair set in wavy lines and his light-blue eyes were quick.

"Counselor Frank A. Potter," somebody whispered in Corky Ellsworth's ear.

The attorney took his place opposite

Colonel Crile and placed his left elbow on his hip, tapping his cheek with his fingers.

"Spit it out, Counselor Potter," ordered the judge.

Potter stared insolently at Colonel Crile who held himself very erect, his lips curled in a sneer. Bad blood between these two, Ellsworth decided.

Corky did not care much about the Mace's legal opponent but when Potter spoke it was with power and logic. Plainly he knew all the tricks of the law.

But the magistrate, on hearing both sides, refused to release the captive on bail.

"They got a watertight case, Potter. I'll set the trial for the fourteenth."

Potter frowned. Here was a man who was used to having his own way.

Spectators had sifted into the courtroom. One was a small man with a round head and sparse brown hair. He wore "city clothes" and looked shirty, a mischief maker. He left before the prisoner was led off by a jailer.

The Mace outfit filed out to find that a crowd had collected. Ellsworth could see at once that the townsfolk hated the Criles, and there were hard looks and mutterings. But Ellsworth was contemptuous of any public prejudice.

"I got business here in town, like I told yuh," he said to Jeff Crile. "I'll see yuh later."

"Better stick with us now!" warned Jeff, but Ellsworth shook his head.

The alert Mace riders mounted and rode off behind the colonel, but Ellsworth stood his ground. He was a free man in a free country, and did not mean to be intimidated.

Boos trailed the Mace. The small man with the round head whom Corky had seen in the courtroom was a leader in this hatred directed toward Crile. Corky only glanced at him contemptuously.

Ellsworth crossed to the Palace, the largest saloon in Mullen City. He went to the bar for a drink but had taken only a sip or two when the little man came in and slid up beside him.

"So yuh're a pard of the Criles!" he drawled.

"What business is it of yores?" demanded Ellsworth coldly.

"Watch yourself! It ain't healthy to love them dirty killers on the Mace. My handle's George Loese and I can tell yuh plenty. Yuh're a stranger here, so I'll give yuh a tip. One good hombre after another has dropped out of sight on Crile's range, dis-

27

appeared like he was swallered. A man who crosses the river ain't likely to come back!"

Ellsworth was angered, thoroughly.

"I don't believe a word yuh say, Loese!" he said hotly. "The Criles are fine folks."

"Hey, fellers," sang out Loese, as he whirled around from the bar. "Here's a feller who loves the Criles!"

There were mutterings, and men drew nearer. Corky Ellsworth saw it plainly now. There was real danger in being a friend of the Mace.

He braced himself for a fight.

CHAPTER III
LONE STAR POWER

At Texas Ranger headquarters in Austin, Captain Bill McDowell regarded with amazement the remains of the chair he had just kicked into splinters.

"Have to put in a requisition for another," he muttered. "That's the sixth this year. They don't make 'em as tough as they used to."

There had been no complaint from higher up because of McDowell's chair bills. Old as he was the captain was worth a great deal more than his salt.

Once he had been a brimstone hellion of a Ranger who had hurled justice into the teeth of outlaws. Now the infirmities of age pinned him to his desk where he sat and, from bits of information reaching him, could visualize what was happening in the far corners of the huge state. But it riled him to be tied to that desk.

Even so, he knew so much about the

methods of evildoers that he could usually diagnose what the enemy's next move would be. He could sense what to do and when to do it and, according to his instincts, the moment for what-and-when had now arrived.

McDowell gave a whistle so shrill that it hurt his own ears. The attendant in the outer office jumped six inches off his stool and landed running toward the captain's door.

"Send Ranger Hatfield here pronto!" bellowed McDowell, and began pacing, which let off a bit of steam.

Soon a soft tread told him that his star Ranger was at hand. McDowell turned, feeling the satisfaction he always did when Jim Hatfield appeared.

Hatfield towered over McDowell, and in his gray-green, long-lashed eyes was a steady, calm light. His broad shoulders tapered to the narrow waist of the true fighting man. His clothing was of the range — blue shirt, leather trousers, spurred boots, Stetson, and a bandanna at his throat.

His heavy Colts rode in oiled holsters, ready for instant use. Those slim hands of his could flash with magic speed, draw and fire even when the enemy had the advantage. There was sureness about Hatfield, the restrained strength of a panther in his rippling muscles.

But it was not sheer physical prowess which had made Jim Hatfield so feared by outlaws and so admired by other people of Texas. Under his black hair was a brain to match his strength, and he could figure out a situation, pull together the loose ends, and through his shrewd tactics force the enemy to surrender.

McDowell knew all this. That was why, having but a handful of officers to police a vast territory, he saved Hatfield for the hard jobs.

"I got a tough one, Hatfield," boomed the old captain, as the Ranger stood before him. "But mebbe yuh like mysteries!"

"Yes suh, Cap'n Bill. Let's have it." His voice was soft and good-humored.

There was a bench along the wall and they sat down on it while McDowell explained.

"Yuh've heard tell of the Mace Ranch south of San Antonio?" he asked. "Belongs to an hombre named Crile?"

"Yes suh." Hatfield nodded. "One of the biggest spreads in Texas."

"I got complaints from down there," said Cap'n Bill. "There's opposition to Crile, and Mullen City's the focal point of it. Crile fought under Lee and Stonewall Jackson and made a brave name in the war, but

31

somethin's sour now. One man after another is said to have dropped out of sight on Mace range. Can't find hide nor hair of 'em.

"It sounds like Crile's riders might be downin' 'em and hidin' the bodies. Simple enough, so far. But I also have a letter from Crile sayin' he can't get justice, that folks are bandin' together to wipe him out. I understand a man's to be tried in Mullen City court for killin' a Mace *vaquero* and both sides are lined up for a real fight. Hard to tell the right and wrong of anything."

"I'll get started right off," said Hatfield.

"There's one more point," McDowell said. "You savvy Joe the Knife."

Hatfield tensed. He knew all about "Joe the Knife," all right, an outlaw Texican who had slain a young Texas Ranger sent out from McDowell's office.

The Rangers never dropped such a matter and there were secret orders to be on the lookout for the killer. Hatfield was aware that the matter had been gnawing at McDowell for many months. The Rangers would never rest until the killing of one of their number was avenged.

Hatfield wondered just what Cap'n Bill's mention of Joe the Knife could have to do with the matter in hand. McDowell told him.

"Remember that lawyer who flimflammed that Border jury into acquitin' Joe the Knife?" the old man growled. "Name of Frank A. Potter? Well he's defendin' that prisoner in Mullen City."

Hatfield understood. So the savage killers had broken from the murky depths of their border hideaway into the clear light of Texas!

McDowell had other information which he passed on to the Ranger. There were two sad letters from widows of Mullen City men who had disappeared on the Mace range. One, a Mrs. Rob Davis, had lost not only her husband but her property.

Armed with all the available facts Hatfield took his leave of McDowell. The old captain stood in the sunbathed doorway and saw the tall Ranger mount the magnificent golden sorrel which carried him on his perilous missions — Goldy, trained for war.

A carbine rode under one of Hatfield's long legs and he carried emergency rations in his bags. Man and horse could live off the country as they campaigned.

McDowell felt a vicarious excitement, seeing a man hunter starting his run.

"Be a bad day for Texas when Hatfield don't come back," he thought.

There was nostalgia in the old Ranger Captain's rheumy eyes as he watched his

Ranger pick up speed, heading south for Mullen City and the mystery of the Mace. . . .

Three days later the Ranger rode into Mullen City. The morning was bright and the sun beat down warmly on the plaza. But instead of the usual sleepy look of such a settlement on a weekday, Mullen City was buzzing with excitement.

Saddled horses stood about, awaiting their owners. Large groups of citizens had collected, some townsmen, and others in range garb. The center of interest seemed to be the courthouse.

The windows and doors of the long building were open to catch what breeze might be stirring. On one side of the main entrance lounged a party of cowboys, some of them Mexican *vaqueros* and the rest Texans. They were heavily armed and, while slouched in apparent ease, they were on the alert.

They eyed the Ranger and he returned their appraising stares. The brand on their mustangs was a clublike design.

"That's the Mace, I reckon," decided Hatfield.

On the other side, and in like watchful attitude, were more men — cowboys and ranchers, townsmen, glaring at the compact group of the big outfit.

Hatfield could feel the danger in the sultry air. In the course of his duties he had at times set charges of explosives and lighted the fuses. Now he experienced the same sensations he had known while awaiting the blasts.

Through the wide doorway Hatfield could see the courtroom. It was packed with sweating spectators. The judge sat on his high bench facing the entrance. In the box was a sallow-faced prisoner, guarded by armed officers. It looked as if the trial of which Cap'n Bill had spoken was about to begin.

Hatfield knew that the best source of information in such a town would be the saloons, so he rode to the largest of the lot.

A sign proclaimed it to be the Palace which also called itself a hotel, since rooms could be rented.

Hatfield left the golden sorrel in the shade and went inside. The bartender was hanging out an open window. He came to serve the tall customer.

"Looks like a big time in the old town," suggested the Ranger as the man set a bottle on the bar.

"Yes, suh!" The barkeeper was so excited he could not keep from glancing out the front window at the plaza. "It's the town and the small ranchers in these parts fightin' Crile's Mace. Been too many fellers killed over there by Crile's riders. We're sick of it."

"Who's on trial?"

"Man named Harry Tate. The Mace caught him and turned him in, claimin' he had downed one of their *vaqueros*. We figger Crile handed Tate over to the law this time to fool folks. Counselor Frank Potter's goin' to give it to the Criles right. Fact is, I aim to go over and listen. I'm watchin' for a pard to signal me when the fireworks start I'll leave the bottle out if yuh want to stay and drink."

"I'll go along," said Hatfield.

Soon the bartender's friend waved from the courthouse window, and the Ranger crossed the square with the Mullen City man. The seats were all taken, so they stood at the rear among others in the hot room.

"That's Potter, the big hombre in the blue pants," the barkeeper told the Ranger. "That peppery old cuss with the beard is Colonel Crile. They hate each other's insides. That hefty youngster with Crile is his son Jeff, and that young cowboy with the light hair is named Ellsworth. He's throwed in with the Criles. They say he's sweet on the colonel's daughter, Lucia."

The magistrate rapped testily with his gavel.

"Order — order in this court!" bawled a man with a star pinned to his shirt. "Court will be cleared if yuh don't keep shut."

Murmurings ceased, and Counselor Potter rose. His very act of standing up was impressive and held all eyes. He turned slowly toward the magistrate and bowed. It was plain he was a skillful actor. Every move he made was perfectly timed.

The lawyer wore a silk shirt and a stock with a flashing diamond stickpin in its folds. His blue trousers were spick-and-span. He had a massive, squarish head and his hair was pomaded. A crisp brown mustache bristled on his lip and his eyes, the color of a high sky, were quick.

"Your Honor and Gentlemen of the Jury," began Potter, in a commanding voice, "you have heard the accusations against this poor lad who has been signaled out by the Mace as Crile's latest victim." The sneer was obvious. "Must I go into the lurid details of our friends from this side of the river who have disappeared on Mace range to satisfy a bloodthirsty egotist's whim? Yes, in this solemn court I accuse Madison Crile of ordering the killings of decent citizens of our community because they dared to tread on his sacred soil! To cap the climax, this mighty despot now asks the law to execute his deadly designs for him!

"Can any sane man — and I can see that you gentlemen are eminently shrewd and clear-thinking — fail to realize what occurred that day when this unfortunate young man was trapped by Crile's gunslingers? Here is the truth! Young Tate came here to raise money to pay off a mortgage on his widowed mother's home.

"He was riding across the Mace when he was set upon by Crile, and he defended himself after they fired on him. He fought to his last bullet and was sorely wounded and taken prisoner. Instead of killing this victim, Crile decided to still the rising voices against the Mace by feigning to consult the law. He brought Tate here, accusing him of shooting a Mace vaquero.

"As for young Ellsworth's story, we have all heard him admit on the stand that he is a friend of the Criles. He is prejudiced, to say the least, and was no doubt excited. The riders he thinks he saw were Mace men trying to kill Harry Tate!"

This was too much for Jeff Crile. He jumped up, his face red.

"Yuh lyin' sidewinder!" he shouted.

"Put that man out!" snapped the judge.

Jeff Crile was hurried from the court by waiting attendants.

Colonel Crile listened in cold silence to Potter. Hostile eyes fixed the Mace owner and outside of his own followers Crile had no sympathizers. Hatfield decided there was no chance of convicting Harry Tate, and Crile evidently realized it, too. The colonel rose and asked the magistrate for permission to be heard.

"I would say," drawled Crile, "that Counselor Potter is as great a liar as he is a coward."

Crile saluted the judge and started from the court. Hatfield saw a flush rising in Potter's cheeks. Crile's dart had struck home. The jury was charged and filed out, but it was a foregone conclusion what the verdict would be.

Hatfield went out into the square as the courtroom began to empty. The Mace outfit had gathered on one side of the plaza and a large crowd faced Crile's fighter's. The colonel steadily watched his enemies. Jeff Crile and the young cowboy Hatfield had heard called Corky Ellsworth were close to the Mace chief.

The Ranger rolled a quirly and observed the scene closely. He noticed a small man with a round head, a shifty-eyed fellow who sifted through the crowd, speaking to one person after another and nodding toward the Criles. He was so busy that he didn't notice when Hatfield moved toward him, came up behind him and paused to listen.

"We ought to show Crile what's what here and now!" the small fellow was saying. "It's time we give the Mace what's comin' to 'em. Let's go after the cusses!"

"Who's that?" asked the Ranger, nudging a nearby citizen and indicating the provocateur.

"Huh? Oh, that's George Loese. Lives in town here."

Loese kept trying to turn the sullen crowd into a lynch mob and make them attack the Mace. He succeeded so well that an angry hum rose until it sounded like the voice of doom.

Then an excited youth stuck his head from an open window to scream:

"Jury's comin' in!"

There was a rush for seats. The Mace waited outside, and Hatfield hung around the doorway.

The jury foreman gave the verdict to the bench. It was "Not Guilty," and on Counselor Potter's face was a smile of triumph.

Harry Tate, the tough who had been acquitted, grinned at men who surged forward to shake hands with him.

That fellow, thought the Ranger, certainly had a mean look.

CHAPTER IV
BLOCKED TRAILS

Derisive shouts announced the verdict to the Criles. Loese was trying afresh to start the mob at the colonel and his outfit.

Hatfield pushed into the crowd. Furiously angry at Loese who was inciting a bloody riot in which lives must be lost, the Ranger was ready to take a hand.

Though on a special mission, it was his duty to check the impending conflict. He preferred to enter a place quietly, without flaunting his authority, so that he might size up a matter before taking action, but this situation called for quick work.

Somehow he must block the mob. It was ten to one against the Mace, yet Crile's riders were heavily armed and their flying lead would account for many men before they were overcome.

"String 'em up!" howled Loese.

With a growing roar, the Mullen City contingent surged toward the Mace.

Colonel Madison Crile sat his big black gelding at the head of his *vaqueros,* a double-barreled shotgun across the pommel of his Mexican saddle. His black eyes were cold and hard as they were fixed on the approaching mob.

Crile moved his hands in a swift gesture and the shotgun muzzles menaced the leaders. They stopped short. Crile raised his voice.

"There will be no trouble unless you start it," he said firmly. "However, if we are attacked we'll defend ourselves."

It was broad daylight, and the Mace men were known to be fighters and the men in the forefront of the crowd knew they would stop the first lead, and that buckshot could scatter and cover a broad space. Loese, who had made certain he was in the rear, yelled furiously:

"Pull the old coot off his hoss! Get him! Rope him!"

Hatfield had by sheer force shoved through the pushing men and was close to Loese. He stuck out a long leg and tripped the man who went down and was trampled by a couple of excited citizens before he could fight back to his feet.

Hatfield had tripped Loese from behind and the little man did not know who had

43

done it. He was too shaken to howl for a moment. And while he spat dirt from his mouth, swearing to himself, Crile was addressing the crowd in a clear voice and the mob quieted. A good sign, thought the Ranger.

"The Mace has been maligned!" Colonel Crile called clearly. "We have done everything possible to please our neighbors, but it isn't enough. We have been attacked and my men have been shot down. After what happened today it is plain that the Mace can't expect justice in the courts here. I intend to defend myself and my own and this is my warning! Keep off Mace range, and if yuh trespass I will take what steps I deem necessary. We are going home now, and if any attempt is made to stop us the blood will be on yore heads."

The readiness of the Mace fighting men sobered the mob. Loese opened his mouth and tried to start the mob going again, but Crile's determined attitude, the guns in the hands of the *vaqueros* and determined Texans checked the attack.

When the crowd no longer showed fight, Crile swept the men with contemptuous eyes and signaled his men. The Mace outfit swung their mustangs and slowly rode toward the ford to cross the river.

"What's the matter?" howled Loese. "Yuh afeared of them cusses?"

His goading had some effect for when Crile and his riders were crossing the stream, yells and jeers rose from some of the mob left behind. A man on one side of the crowd fired a revolver, the shot going wild in the warm air.

Colonel Crile turned in his saddle and sent bullets whirling over the plaza — warnings only. The mob hastily broke up and sought shelter, those who didn't head for the saloons. Throats were dry from the heat and dust and so much shouting.

The Ranger heaved a sigh of relief. After all, he had not been forced to show his hand in Mullen City.

He waited while Potter emerged from the courthouse with Harry Tate, the man whom the lawyer had defended. The two went to the Palace together, trailed by a band of supporters. Soon the court was empty save for a couple of Mexicans sweeping the floor, so Hatfield also pushed into the Palace where Frank Potter was enjoying a drink and his victory over Crile.

Everybody was talking over the exciting events. It was simple enough to nudge a nearby citizen and listen while the whole story was expounded. When Hatfield had learned as much as he could about both sides of the case, he went out and saw to Goldy, leaving the sorrel at a livery stable corral down the street.

He had a hearty meal in the Texas Lunch while from its front window he watched the center of Mullen City. He was getting acquainted with the locale and sizing up those with whom he must deal.

Besides the main trouble between the Mace and the big outfit's neighbors, McDowell had posed another problem. Frank Potter had defended one Joe the Knife, killer of a Texas Ranger. There must be a connection between the attorney and his former client, perhaps only in Potter's records, but something through which it might be possible to track the man who had slain a Ranger. Hatfield meant to have a try at it.

The Ranger's alert mind was busy. If Jeff Crile and Corky Ellsworth had told the truth under oath on the stand, then Harry Tate must have friends in the broken region to the north of the Mace grazing range — and men who hung out there were known not to be above reproach. Then there was the mystery of decent men who had dropped out of sight on Crile's ranch. Hatfield considered it. Some basis must exist

46

for the complaints against the Mace. Often there was jealousy between a big ranch and smaller neighbors. There would be strayed cattle, and the ownership of unbranded calves might be disputed, perhaps outright rustling by a few who thought such a man as Crile could well afford to lose bunches of beefs.

A man of Crile's disposition and pride could lose patience, and might order his riders to shoot first and ask questions afterward. Yet why had Crile turned in such an obvious rascal as Harry Tate instead of ordering him shot, if he had done as Crile claimed? Had Potter been right in claiming that Crile had grown alarmed at the rising cry against the Mace and had tried to prove he was on the side of law and order?

"I'm goin' to trail Tate," decided Hatfield. "If he has pards, like the Criles say, he'll go back to 'em sooner or later."

The excitement and crowds in town due to the trial had been to the Ranger's advantage. It had been made possible for him to enter Mullen City and learn what details he had gathered without drawing undue attention to himself. He hoped his luck would hold. He had Goldy saddled again and at a nearby hitchrack — just in case.

It was no trouble to keep an eye on Harry

Tate through the rest of the afternoon and evening, for the acquitted man spent the time in the Palace, drinking until he could no longer stand up. Tate was laid out on a bench where he snored until the saloon closed at midnight.

Potter and another man supported Tate between them and went up the street. Not far from the Palace stood a red building, a square structure connected to a larger house in back by a covered passage. The front was Potter's law office as proclaimed by his shingle, and evidently the counselor had his living quarters in the rear, for a light came on inside. Potter and the man helping disappeared into the building with Tate.

Hatfield slipped around the other side of the building, to the living quarters. The windows were open to the warm night, and looking through he saw Potter shaking Harry Tate. The drunken man sat slumped in a chair with his eyes shut. The other man was gone.

"Wake up!" growled Potter. "You've had a big evenin' but I'm worn out. You leave town before daylight, savvy? You hear me? This is important. I want you to give this note to Joe."

"All right, all right," muttered Tate. He was still foggy, but the sleep in the saloon had somewhat restored him. "I got to have a hoss and gun."

"Help yourself from my stable. There's a six-shooter and cartridge belt on the peg over there."

Potter handed Tate a folded paper which Tate placed in a pocket.

The listening officer was interested. There must be a strong bond between this lawyer and his client since Potter gave Tate a horse and a gun and asked for no payment. The Ranger would have liked to see the letter which was to be given to "Joe." The name, in connection with Potter, might mean a great deal. Of course there were plenty of Joes, but Joe the Knife who had shot down a Texas Ranger had escaped punishment, thanks to Potter.

"I'm turnin' in," announced Potter, yawning. "Watch out when you cross the Mace. They may shoot you this time, and you won't need a trial."

Tate grinned. His yellow buck teeth accented the crookedness in his sallow face.

"Yuh sure made a fool out of that cuss Crile, counselor."

Potter's ego was flattered. He was a vain man.

"I'll make Crile pay," he promised grimly. Nodding to Harry Tate, he went into

49

another room where he lit a candle and made ready for bed. For a time Tate sat there, pulling himself together. He helped himself to a bracer from Potter's bottle on the sideboard.

It was after one o'clock when the sallow-faced Harry rose and went to the stable. By the light of a lantern he saddled a chestnut gelding. The Ranger watched from the bushes on the side yard. But Hatfield had moved to the shadows under the long sun awnings on Main Street when Tate rode to the plaza out of a lane, rode on out of Mullen City and toward the river.

When Tate crossed at a ford, Hatfield, on Goldy, followed. The Ranger let the man move out ahead, for the range was rolling and open. And he was certain he would be able to pick up Tate's trail when dawn came.

In the first light of the new day the tall man on the golden sorrel stared up at the rising country where hills and rocks loomed over the north sections of the mighty Mace.

The mustang which Tate rode threw his left forehoof a bit and there were two easily identifiable marks imprinted by the hind shoes of the animal. The earth was well-packed and there was a breeze blowing so that the sign would not linger too long. But Hatfield was not far behind Harry Tate who had entered the woods about an hour before.

The skillful tracker kept watching ahead for there was always a chance that such a man as Tate on reaching cover might take precautions to see if he was being followed.

The Mace, Hatfield saw, stretched south and southwest in fine, grassy range. Here and there small breaks occurred — rock upthrusts which were islands in the vast land-ocean. In the distance little groups and black dots were grazing cattle. Once Hatfield's keen eye recognized a running band of mustangs.

More than once he saw — and frowned as he read — signs on pine posts which warned:

KEEP OFF
YOU ARE ON MACE RANGE!

"Mighty fine range they got, Goldy," murmured Hatfield.

The hilly, heavily forested sections on the north would break the winds and storms and protect the grazing areas. It was into this dark country that Harry Tate had plunged.

The sun was warm as it came up behind the Ranger. The sorrel's handsome hide glistened and Goldy switched his long tail and rippled his mane.

"What's up?" inquired Hatfield.

Who-oosh!

The Ranger pulled on his reins to turn the sorrel off as he heard the threatening song of a bullet from a heavy rifle. And as he glanced swiftly about, he knew instantly that the slug had come from one of the clumps of rock and bush about three hundred yards away. He gave Goldy a bit of knee pressure and the trained sorrel picked up speed and zigzagged away from there. Another bullet kicked up the dirt fifty feet alongside them and ricocheted, screaming off into the air.

"They're mighty wide," grunted the Ranger, looking back over a shoulder.

Men came from the other side of the rocks, pulling saddled horses with them and leaping to saddles to pelt after him. There were about six in the party. He knew he could outride them but it would force him off his course. Tate's trail would grow cold and he might find trouble in following it when he reached the hills. The gunfire could warn Tate.

A couple of the men after Hatfield wore Mexican steeple sombreros and short jackets with tight-fitting pants. The others looked to be Texas cowhands, all of them excellent horsemen.

CHAPTER V
CLOSE CALL

For a time Hatfield thought he might reach the wooded district by fast riding, since Goldy was too fleet for his pursuers to overtake him. But as he neared the uneven line of trees and rocks a second party broke from cover and came straight at him, whooping it up and shooting over him. There were ten men in this bunch.

Hatfield had to veer and run northeast, which would eventually bring him back to the river.

A few minutes later several riders emerged from an arroyo which the Ranger had skirted on his way across the range. They had evidently been moving through it and they surged up onto the plain and spurred in a direction to cut him off.

"We're boxed," he muttered.

The other two parties had spread out now and were driving him hard. He kept on at full-tilt, determined to blast his way through with his guns. He was certain that the men who were after him were friends of Harry Tate and having spied him trailing Tate, had come for him.

There were only four in the third group and he picked this thin line for his attempt. He would shoot his way out if he had to.

The powerful golden sorrel tore on and the wind whipped at the strapped Stetson covering the black hair on the tall officer's head.

Hatfield was closing on the four who had emerged from the arroyo and he was about to draw his Colt and shoot his way through when he recognized who they were. He had come near enough to make out the spade goatee and mustache and the general lines of Colonel Madison Crile.

He realized suddenly that these men were not Tate's questionable comrades but Mace riders!

And he was trespassing.

Hatfield raised his arm in the universal gesture of peace, asking for a parley. He left his guns in their holsters and slowed the sorrel a bit. Mace fighters were sweeping in on him from all sides, but he preferred to take a chance with Crile, after what he had seen of the outfit in Mullen City.

Colonel Crile instantly replied to the

Ranger's signal. He bawled a command to his men and waved a gauntleted hand back and forth before his face to stop the firing of the other two groups on the Ranger's trail.

Hatfield came within hailing distance and sang out:

"Tell yore boys to keep off, Crile! I don't want to hurt anybody!"

He would not surrender, to the Mace or anyone else, but he had no desire to fight the outfit — yet. So far he had uncovered no evidence to prove that Crile had broken the law, but he wanted to be sure before he took decisive steps.

Madison Crile had a trained soldier's courage. He waved his riders back and came straight at Hatfield, who pulled up and carefully kept his hands in sight so that the Mace outfit might not misconstrue any motions he made. Crile's black eyes were penetrating as they took in the size and obvious power of the big fellow.

"We missed yore friend Harry Tate," said Crile grimly. "But we have you."

Yet it was more of a question than an accusation and Hatfield so accepted it.

"Tate's no pard of mine, Colonel Crile."

Crile was sizing him up. The colonel was a shrewd man and had been in the habit of commanding large numbers of men. Certainly he must be able to read character in a face and what he saw in Hatfield's rugged features and steady gray-green eyes impressed him just as it had so many other decent people, men and women alike.

The Ranger was prepared to fight it out if the Mace opened the ball, though the whole line behind him had pulled up and sat their saddles, ready with guns to back up their chief. But Hatfield hoped it would not come to that.

"I saw yuh in the mob at the courthouse yesterday," said Crile.

"That's right," drawled Hatfield. "I'd just pulled in. My first visit to Mullen City."

Colonel Crile was silent for a moment. Hatfield was fully aware of the armed men at his back. Once as he gave a quick glance around, he saw that Jeff Crile and Corky Ellsworth were present.

"If yuh're an honest man," asked Crile, "what are yuh doin' on my range? Didn't yuh see my warnin' signs?"

"Yes, suh, I saw several of 'em," admitted the Ranger. "A man would have to be blind to miss 'em. But I had business over this way."

He made up his mind that he must explain his presence to Crile, and how to do it. The fact that he was following Harry Tate would fit in nicely.

"I hope yuh'll keep it under yore hat, suh, but I'm a deputy sheriff down here to arrest Harry Tate for the shootin' he done in San Antonio. I was trailin' him when yore *vaqueros* gave him a run. Till I recognized you I believed Tate's pards were chasin' me."

He felt the black eyes weighing him, knew that Crile was turning over what he had said.

"I don't like strangers on my range," Crile said slowly. "But since yuh're here with an honest purpose I'll cooperate. Let me see yore papers."

The Ranger was not prepared for this. He did not wish to expose his true identity to Crile or anyone else at the moment.

"They're in my room at the Palace in Mullen City," he replied glibly. "I ain't fool enough to carry 'em on me, for if Tate and his gang caught me with my badge and credentials I'd be a goner."

Colonel Crile stared straight at him. His curved nostrils flared. "In that case," he said, "I'll ask yuh to leave my ranch. When yuh can prove yore assertions, suh, please come to my home and I'll do everything in my power to assist yuh."

Hatfield shrugged. There was no sense in

continuing his attempt to trail Tate for the Mace had wrecked his chances. Tate must have heard the shooting if he had not seen the chase from the upper woods, and would have covered his tracks well by now.

"All right, Colonel Crile. I'll be ridin'."

They gave way before him at Crile's signal and the Ranger trotted the sorrel toward the river, which formed the Mace's eastern boundary. When he glanced back from time to time he saw *vaqueros* following him at a distance to make sure he obeyed Crile's orders.

"Anyhow, I'm alive and kickin'," he told the sorrel.

He had been caught on Mace range but Crile had proved decent enough under the circumstances. There might well be two sides to this controversy, after all. From what Hatfield had observed in Mullen City the Mace had cause for complaint against some of their neighbors.

Goldy breasted the stream and shook the water from his haunches after reaching the east bank, with Mullen City close at hand. Hatfield rode down the highway, past pleasant homes in their yards, one of which had a wooden sign reading, "Rob Davis." He gave it a second glance, for he had not forgotten that McDowell had had a letter from the widow of this man who had been lost when he had crossed Mace range. . . .

Mullen City bustled in the warm morning sunshine. Housewives were shopping at the stores and the anvil in the blacksmith's shop rang with the strokes of the hammer as a shoe was shaped. Children played in the plaza and chickens, pigs and dogs were about. Counselor Frank Potter's office was open and as Hatfield slowly passed he could see the lawyer through the open windows. Along the street there were loafers on the benches, playing idly with their clasp knives or whittling, half-asleep.

"So yuh took a ride across the Mace!" someone said sharply.

Hatfield swung his gray-green eyes. Standing by a thick post was George Loese, the small man who had tried to incite riot after the trial of Harry Tate. Loese's dark pants were tucked into stringless shoes, a stained white shirt was open at the throat, and a straw hat was pushed back on his round head. Sparse brown hair stuck to his sweated brow. It was plain that he was decidedly curious about the tall man who had just crossed the river.

The Ranger nodded and turned the sorrel into the rack. He got down and scowled back toward the Mace range.

"Some day those cusses 'll get what they got comin'," he snarled.

"What happened?" inquired Loese. "Did they gun yuh?"

"Yes, suh! If I didn't have a fast hoss I'd be buzzard bait, I reckon."

Hatfield's attitude and look were so tough that Loese was pleased and impressed, with no idea that the Ranger was dissembling, acting for his benefit. Hatfield had quickly decided that there was no telling when he might make use of Loese, whose active bitterness toward the Criles was so plain.

"If I had my say," declared Loese in a loud voice, "decent folks would band together and kill off them vermin." He lowered his voice to ask the tall stranger: "Come on in and have one on me."

The Ranger ducked under the rail and the two entered the Palace Bar. Loese bought a round, then Hatfield treated. They parted with mutual compliments, the Ranger to take care of Goldy and leave the sorrel at the livery stable corral as before. Hatfield was tired and needed sleep. He ate a hearty meal and retired to his room on the second floor of the Palace.

It was night when the Ranger awoke, refreshed and ready to go to work again. Mullen City hummed in the pleasant evening, the saloons filled. Music came from downstairs in the Palace.

Hatfield pulled on his boots, strapped on his belts, and set his Stetson. He went downstairs to the saloon where gilt oil lamps hung from rafters to fight the bar. Sawdust shifted under the tall man's weight. At the counter with a foot on the brass rail stood the counselor, Potter, George Loese and others Hatfield had seen around town, among them the judge and most of the jury at Tate's trial.

Loese grinned and winked at the big Ranger, who gave the small man a nod. This attracted Potter's attention. In the mirror behind the bar Hatfield saw Potter ask Loese a question, and Loese replied, no doubt explaining who Hatfield was.

The Ranger was determined to probe deeply into Frank Potter's operations, for there was the matter of the slain Texas Ranger and Joe the Knife, as well as the present situation with Potter the leading opponent to Crile's Mace. Hatfield preferred to force issues when he could, and he had no intention now of waiting around for the enemy to strike again.

He kept an eye on Potter without being obtrusive. The lawyer ate a late supper in the annex next to the Palace bar. He had a pretty girl for company and seemed in no hurry to return home. About ten o'clock Hatfield strolled up the sidewalk past Potter's home and office. The office was dark, but a lamp was burning in the living quarters.

The Ranger made his preparations and waited around until midnight. Then Potter came home and turned in, for soon the place was dark.

Hatfield had a small bull's-eye lantern ready. Since the office was separated from Potter's rooms by that narrow connecting passage, he believed he could work up front without waking Potter, providing the lawyer was asleep. He gave Potter time to drift off, then quietly raised a window on the shadowed office wall. He climbed in and squatted there, letting his eyes grow accustomed to the gloom. A shaft of light from the street lantern helped.

Across from him stood a large square filing cabinet made of wood. The Ranger moved the slide of the bull's-eye lantern a bit and focused his light on the cabinet. It had four big drawers. They were neatly labelled. One was equipped with a padlock and marked: "CONFIDENTIAL."

It took fifteen minutes to work out the hasp screws from the wood without making sounds that might disturb Potter. Hatfield inched the drawer out, and used his slit of light. Folders were carefully inscribed. From what he read he gathered that most had to do with clients Potter had defended. He hunted for Joe the Knife's record. After a search he drew out a folder with the name Jos. Carmozo on it and examined it.

The record said:

"Alias Joe the Knife." This man will do anything for money. He has killed at least a dozen victims, in El Paso, Austin, and is wanted in Kansas and New Mexico for murder. Shot Texas Ranger Drew Ince to death on July 18, 1876, in Brownsville, and acquitted by jury August 24th.

There was more on Joe the Knife, enough to hang the Border ruffian every day of the week.

Hatfield tried the T's. Sure enough, there was Harry Tate's record as a highwayman and rustler.

George Loese was ticketed;

No good for strongarm work but excellent for underground operations. Cowardly in battle. Loese hails from New Orleans where he knifed a man in the back and fled to Texas.

The Ranger had run into a gold mine for a law officer. Potter had all this detailed information on his clients, and no doubt was making use of it.

In the back of the private drawer was a folder marked "Deeds." Curiously Hatfield took it out and thumbed through the documents. A name caught his eyes: "Robert Davis to Frank A. Potter." It was a quit-claim deed to the Davis property in Mullen City.

And there were others. Next the land deeds was correspondence labelled "Private." Hatfield was just growing deeply immersed in a series of letters between Potter and a Z-N Manufacturing Company of San Antonio when his keen ears caught noises outside. Quickly he shut off the lantern.

He crouched in the darkness, listening. There were men moving around Potter's place. He could hear their soft treads and the sounds of subdued voices. And in the living quarters at the rear, Potter was stirring.

"Better get out of here," decided Hatfield.

As he straightened up the street door opened. Against the glow from outside a tall figure stopped in the entry.

"You there, Potter?" called the fellow. He had an unpleasant, penetrating voice. "Seen yore light. Yuh sent for us?"

Chapter VI
Dangerous Hours

More men were behind the fellow with the strident voice, and someone struck a match to light a cigarette. The flare showed the tall leader, lean as a fence rail in leather pants and shirt and high spurred boots. A steeple sombrero was canted on his narrow head with the strap loose in the runner.

He was brown of skin and had recently shaved so that the long white knife scar slanting across his left cheek stood out, this disfigurement pulling up a corner of his mouth. His eyes were set deep over a hawk nose, and the bony hands at the ends of the long, thin arms were oversized, with spatulate fingertips.

In a slumped belt rode a black-stocked Colt revolver. A sheath held a fine knife with silver filagree patterns in the horn handle, a weapon such as a breed would fancy at close quarters.

"Joe the Knife!" decided the Ranger. He

had never seen the outlaw but McDowell's description had been perfect. Potter had overheard Joe the Knife's low hail for the counselor called from the rear:

"Are you in the office, Joe?"

"What in tarnation!" exclaimed Joe. "Who's that over there?" There was a shuffling of booted feet. "Strike a light, Marty!" ordered the lanky bandit.

Hatfield was ready. They had glimpsed that moving bull's-eye slit as they had approached Potter's. Joe the Knife had taken it for granted that the counselor was working in his office and the open door showed the outlaws had been expected by the lawyer. But now they were suspicious.

"Potter!" called Joe. "Come in here!"

A door in back opened and a heavy step shook the flimsy connecting passage. It was Hatfield's last chance and he snatched at it, jumping across the office in a couple of bounds. A match scratched where Joe the Knife stood among his men.

"Halt, whoever yuh be!" bawled Joe the Knife and a revolver cluck-clucked as it was cocked.

Potter flung open the second connecting door to the office.

"What's goin' on?" he demanded. "You're

67

makin' enough racket to wake the whole town!"

"I thought you was workin' in here," Joe the Knife answered. "Who in blazes is it?"

Marty's wooden match came up. The Ranger threw a hasty slug at the men bunched around the Knife and hoped it would give him the moments he must have to escape. The bony breed fired, but his bullet kicked up splinters from the floor. One of the outlaws began to yelp in pain, slashed by a Ranger missile. The match flickered out and Hatfield dived from the open window, his long legs scraping the sill.

So far none had had more than a vague glimpse of the shadowy, tall figure. Joe the Knife had withheld his fire because he had believed it was Potter in the office, but now they were aware an intruder had been there. Another match flamed as six-shooters jumped to calloused hands and blazed away at the window through which the snooper had gone.

Potter jumped to the logical conclusion.

"It's a Crile spy! Get him, boys! Look — he's been at my private files. Kill him!" There was a frantic shrillness to the lawyer's usually deep voice.

Hatfield had hit the dirt hard and landed bunched up. He flung himself to one side, rolling off before he jumped up and ran as fast as he could toward the rear of the place.

"After him, you fools!" raged Potter.

They had lost precious seconds getting started after the running Ranger. He came to the corner of the house, turned it, and made for the beaten path to where Potter kept his horses. Glancing back when he reached the shadowed side of the barn he saw hurrying figures just emerging from the kitchen door on his trail.

With the stable between himself and his angry enemies the Ranger dodged past the end of a high board fence, across a house yard on the adjoining street, vaulted another fence and reached the adobe wall of a darkened feed store. He stopped here to get his breath, and see if they had been able to trail him.

The shots and cries had awakened the neighbors around Potter's and a couple of candles in upstairs windows flickered up.

Evidently the hubbub did not please Potter for after the first flurry of noise, Joe the Knife and his men continued the hunt for their quarry quietly. Pressed into a dark doorway, the Ranger saw a couple of them emerge from the narrow lane through which he had come. They stood on the wooden walk and looked up and down. Hatfield never moved, hidden in his recess.

"He didn't come this way," he heard one outlaw say to the other.

They turned and went back toward Potter's.

When they had gone Hatfield slid his Colt into its holster and walked up Main Street. He crossed between street lights and made the plaza above the courthouse. A big oak tree offered concealment and he leaned against it and watched as Joe the Knife and his men flitted through the town.

The Palace Saloon & Hotel was dark except for a low night lamp burning in an entryway. Joe the Knife and two gun-slingers came rapidly along the sidewalk from Potter's, the others having difficulty in keeping up with the lanky killer's long-legged gait. Leaning against the trunk of the oak, Hatfield observed them as they passed under a light.

"I'd like to give yuh what yuh got comin', Joe," he thought. "But you'll get yours — and right now there's bigger fish in sight. Mebbe I'll hook Potter through yuh."

He thought he might be able to pick off Joe the Knife at once, and be through with it, but a miss would betray his position. And there seemed to be plenty of enemy fighters around town at the present moment.

These were dangerous hours for Hatfield, as he jockeyed for position. It was vital that he determine the motives of both sides in the case he had undertaken for Captain McDowell before he took positive action. Justice must be done, for that was the Rangers' creed. But he must live in order to mete out justice, and a chance slug could terminate anybody's career. Several had come mighty close to Ranger Hatfield as he had checked up on counselor Frank Potter that night.

He was feeling satisfied that he had eluded his pursuers when he saw Joe the Knife suddenly reach out and pull back his two companions. They ducked into the dark mouth of a space between two buildings.

"Now what?" wondered the alert Ranger. What could be the cause of a move like that?

His gray-green eyes swept the street. The excitement due to the shooting had quickly died out, and Potter's neighbors had been reassured and returned to bed. The plaza and roads were deserted.

From comfortable elation at having outdodged Joe the Knife and Potter, the Ranger was plunged into a state of anxiety as he saw a tall figure mount the Palace porch and enter the open doorway. The man was silhouetted for a moment against the light burning on the counter in the hotel.

"Corky Ellsworth!" muttered Hatfield.

One of Joe the Knife's aides slipped from the passage and ran up the sidewalk. Plainly he was headed for Potter's to fetch plenty of assistance, so they could surround the Palace and have Ellsworth in the bag. This was obvious to the watching Ranger. He could no longer see Ellsworth in the little lobby. The cowboy had gone on further into the hotel.

"They'll figger it was Ellsworth in Potter's office, shore as it's hot below!" Hatfield decided.

After what he had come across in Potter's files he knew that the counselor would never allow the suspected spy to escape. Ellsworth would die the moment they caught him. Somehow the Ranger must snatch Ellsworth from Potter and Joe the Knife.

He had not a long time in which to determine his moves. It would be only a few minutes until Potter's gunfighters had the Palace in a ring of guns. Hatfield was already on the run down the plaza, on the way to a place below the hotel where he could get across and dodge through to the back street. He made it like a flitting shadow.

The back door of the big saloon stood

open. Skirting piles of rusting tin cans he entered. A hall led to the front and he saw Corky Ellsworth coming down the stairs which led to the sleeping rooms on the second floor. The tall cowpuncher had a puzzled look on his young face.

"Ellsworth!" Hatfield called softly. "This way, pronto!"

Corky started, and a hand flicked to his six-shooter as he heard Hatfield's hail. He glanced over the banister and stopped.

"Say, I was huntin' you, Sheriff," he began in a conversational tone. "Colonel Crile sent me. We had to make it quiet and late at night because the Mace has a lot of enemies in this town."

"Dry up!" snapped Hatfield. "We got about thirty seconds to make the back door, Ellsworth. C'mon!"

Ellsworth blinked. But the tall officer was already gliding away and Corky vaulted the rail and ran after him.

"What's the matter?" inquired Corky.

"Joe the Knife and a couple of dozen gun-fanners are huntin' you," replied Hatfield hastily. "Have yore Colt ready. Where's yore hoss?"

"Jeff Crile's holdin' him south of the ford."

Hatfield reached the back door and paused to check up, gun in hand. Ellsworth looked back along the hall to the lobby.

"There he is!"

Joe the Knife and three men with pistols up had rushed into the Palace and sighted Ellsworth. Hatfield was outside, turning down the back street. Joe had started in a few seconds ahead of the hurrying fighters who were coming down the back street.

Bullets began humming at Ellsworth and the Ranger from two directions. Hatfield ran lightly on, with Corky at his heels. The Ranger made a turn and cut back toward Main.

"Be ready, now!" he warned. "They may be thick in the street."

Ellsworth was still mystified but he had heard the enemy lead and was aware that the supposed deputy had saved his life. He followed instructions without question. They pelted across the walk, ducked under the rail, and ran down the street. A yell came from near the Palace and again they were fired on.

"You and Crile ride south along the east bank of the river!" ordered Hatfield. "I'll overtake yuh pronto."

"All right, Sheriff."

Ellsworth rushed on, and the Ranger dodged around the livery stable. Goldy was waiting for him in the corral. He snatched his saddle and mounted bareback, moving down the rutted dirt lane with all speed possible.

Out of town he paused to saddle and cinch up his leather seat. Resuming his run he heard gunshots toward the gleaming ribbon of the stream. He kept going parallel to the river and picking up speed. Half an hour later he breathed a sigh of relief as he realized that Joe the Knife and his men had given up the chase as hopeless in the night. Soon he heard a hail. Corky Ellsworth and Jeff Crile were not far off.

Hatfield rolled a quirly, after checking up. The water purled over a series of low rock ledges, making a pleasing sound and the brush cast black shadows. Across was the Mace range, and there were smaller ranches south and southeast, with Mullen City well above them.

"What happened, anyways?" inquired Ellsworth.

"It was like this," drawled the Ranger. "I was standin' in the plaza mindin' my own business when I saw you go into the Palace. I knowed yuh, since yuh was pointed out to me at the trial, and then yuh was with the Criles yesterday. I heard 'em say they was out to get yuh, and I could see they had yuh boxed so I horned in."

75

"Will yuh shake hands?" asked Ellsworth gravely. "I shore am grateful. Jeff, now I savvy how you felt when I opened up on them gunslingers that day."

Hatfield reached out and felt Ellsworth's firm hand pressure, expressing the cowboy's deep gratitude. The burly Jeff loomed large on his horse, his eyes glowing as he stared at the tall officer.

"What's yore handle, Sheriff?" he inquired.

"Hays, Jim Hays. I reckon yuh know my business. I told yore father I was after Harry Tate for a killin' done in San Antonio. But he run me off his range."

"Dad thought it over," said Crile. "That's why we're here. He sent us to find yuh. The Mace needs help and mebbe you can give it to us."

"Will yuh ride to the ranch with us?" asked Ellsworth. "We can talk it over better and the colonel's waitin' for yuh."

"Suits me. Lead the way."

"Have yuh got yore papers with yuh this time?" Jeff Crile wanted to know.

Ellsworth was impatient. "He don't need any papers or anything else with me, Jeff! He saved my bacon. Let's ride!"

CHAPTER VII
PLEA FOR HELP

Gray of a new day was behind Hatfield and his two saddle companions when they pulled up at the ranch house. Hatfield could make out the shapes of the roomy *hacienda,* the bunkhouse, cabins, sheds and barns, shops and all that was needed for such an establishment.

An armed *vaquero* in a steeple sombrero had challenged them as they had come along the trail toward the Mace, and there was another sentinel on the alert in the yard by the house. Jeff Crile answered the challenges in Spanish and as the Mace guards had been on the lookout for them they were quickly passed.

"We can't take any chances," explained young Crile. "The Mace has plenty enemies, Sheriff Hays."

The big house was darkened for the night and the family sound asleep. Hatfield was tired, and so were his two young companions. The Ranger was glad, after they had groomed their horses, to turn in at the bunkhouse for a few hours.

The sun was brilliant in an azure sky when Hatfield rose and made his toilet at the watering-trough in the side yard. He rolled a quirly and his nostrils widened at the scent of coffee in the clean air. He was hungry. So were Corky Ellsworth and Jeff Crile as they emerged, yawning.

"Breakfast'll taste mighty *bueno*," grunted Jeff.

He took stock of last night's companions in the light of day. Young Crile had a fine head and good features, clean brown eyes and obvious strength of body and mind. His black hair curled around his prominent ears with a virility of its own that was matched in his entire makeup.

Hatfield had liked Corky Ellsworth at sight. He liked him still better on closer acquaintance. The cowboy was tall and lean, and his smile caught hold. His eyes were blue and forward looking and his light hair crisp.

Life was fun for such young men. It might be dangerous at times, but they enjoyed it. Hatfield relaxed as they jested together and played like colts.

"I could eat a hoss," declared Corky.

"Yuh're goin' to, if the steak's no better than Juanita cooked it yesterday," said Jeff. "I'm starvin'. Let's eat."

Meat, cakes, and a great pot of steaming coffee were served to the three, by Mexican women who ran the Mace kitchen. It was a late breakfast for they had overslept, not having turned in until near dawn.

There were a few cowboys around, Mexicans and Texans. They were armed, and were either guards or wranglers. Brown children in cotton shirts played about, offspring of the large number of Mexican women employees who did the cleaning, cooking and other domestic chores for the Mace.

Hatfield was impressed by the size of the outfit and its self-sufficiency. He had often heard of the big ranch, but this was his first visit to Crile's, and the place was much larger than he had imagined it to be.

After they had smoked, Jeff led the tall officer through to his father's office in the front of the house. Elegant furnishings, thick rugs, fine paintings, furniture imported from Old Spain and other parts of Europe, filled the shadowed rooms of the *hacienda*. A patio in which shade trees and flowers grew showed through the inner windows.

When Jeff ushered Hatfield into the office, Colonel Madison Crile sat at his desk. There was a good deal of paper work and correspondence connected with the running of such a ranch. The colonel rose and his penetrating black eyes were riveted on the Ranger.

"Welcome to the Mace, suh," he said.

His hat lay on the desk, his fine head of silver hair, matching his goatee and mustache, uncovered. His slender body had a ramrod's carriage and his chin was up. Grim lines etched his face.

"Thanks, suh," drawled the Ranger.

"Corky ran into a mess in town," Jeff said to his father. "Sheriff Hays pulled him out of it."

"That's right, suh," spoke up Ellsworth eagerly. He had followed the other two into the office. "I'll ride the river with Hays any time."

Colonel Crile nodded, then gave his son and Ellsworth a meaning glance. The two hastily retired, closing the door after them.

"Please have a chair, Sheriff," begged the colonel. "A Cuban cheroot? Whisky or *tequila?*"

Hatfield refused the drink, so soon after breakfast, but accepted the smoke. The colonel also lighted up. The sun streamed in at the broad windows through which Crile could look out on his vast range. It was a pleasant outlook.

"Yuh're a guest in my home, Sheriff Hays, and at my request," began Crile. "I hope yuh'll feel no offense if I ask to see yore credentials. The situation here is so dangerous that I can take no chances whatsoever."

Hatfield returned Crile's straight gaze. "To tell yuh the truth, I have no deputy's papers with me this trip. Yuh'll have to take me at my word, Colonel Crile. I'll say this. I'm shore on the side of decent folks, and so far I've seen nothin' to prove the Mace ain't on the same footin'."

Crile was disappointed at failing to see the supposed deputy's papers. He kept watching the tall man across from him. Evidently he had been deeply impressed by their first meeting, out on the Mace north range.

"I'll have to accept yuh and I will," said Colonel Crile finally. "We're in deep trouble here. The Mace has been blamed for killin's we never took part in. Will yuh believe me when I say that my *vaqueros* and cowboys have strict orders to shoot only when attacked?"

Hatfield nodded. "I might believe it. Yet they opened up on me, Colonel."

"Over yore head as a warnin'," declared

Crile. "We also believed yuh to be one of Harry Tate's friends since yuh followed him so closely."

Hatfield shrugged. He waited for Crile to show his hand. As yet he was not certain of the Mace and he wished to be so before he told his true identity.

"I have written complaints to the Texas Rangers," went on Crile. Deep lines in his brow showed his tenseness and the worry he had been through. "The trouble we've had is growing and soon will be out of hand. Men that I used to be friendly with, good citizens of Mullen City, and owners of smaller ranches on the east bank of the river, are ready to shoot at the Mace. It's come up rapidly, it seems to me. I don't know why. Ever since I spoke with yuh. Hays, I've had yuh on my mind. Yuh impressed me as a man with real power and ability to think.

"You are a law officer. I have an idea. I want yuh to assume the job of ferretin' out our trouble and bringin' whoever's responsible to justice. The Mace hasn't spirited men away. Then who has? Will yuh accept the position? I'll gladly pay any expenses yuh incur and whatever salary yuh state."

Hatfield did not immediately accept, nor did he refuse the offer. Instead, he asked a question.

"Tell me what Frank Potter has against yuh, Colonel?"

Crile jumped and his eyes narrowed.

"Yuh're as smart as a whip, ain't yuh? I felt it. Yes, Potter hates me. We were opponents in the War Between the States. But that would never touch the honor of gentlemen. However it so happened that in battle I saw Potter tuck his tail between his legs and desert his company. He was an officer, which makes it much worse.

"A while later, I captured Potter skulkin' in the woods. He cried and begged for mercy in a disgustin' manner. This was near the end of the war and soon he was released. My next encounter with him was in Mullen City. He undertakes to defend rustlers and worse, and he persecutes the Mace. He takes joy in seein' me humiliated and defeated."

"I savvy."

Hatfield thought it over. That there was a personal enmity between Crile and Potter he had already sensed. This would explain Potter's hatred of the Mace owner, yet it hardly cleared up the mystery of missing citizens who had ventured on the big ranch's domain.

"And will yuh accept my offer?" pressed Crile.

"That I can't do," replied the Ranger. "But I'll guarantee to do everything possible to clear up yore trouble. How about Harry Tate and the hombres hidin' in the hills on yore north range?"

The owner of the Mace was obviously disappointed that the big man refused to sign up as the Mace's special investigator. But he put a polite face on the matter.

"They're well-hidden in there," Crile nodded. "We've hunted for 'em to some extent, but it's mighty thick when yuh get off the open range."

"Have yuh thought it might be these outlaws who shoot down and hide the bodies of folks from across the river?"

"It occurred to me."

Hatfield learned what Madison Crile could tell him. It boiled down to the fact that the Mace was being persecuted and could not get justice in the courts. Long range shots had been taken at Crile and his men, and only after the trouble had begun had Crile posted his property.

"Will yuh supply me with fightin' men if and when I need same?" asked Hatfield.

The colonel nodded again. "As long as I'm shore the cause is just, suh." There was some reserve in his manner since the officer had rejected Crile's offer of employment.

Hatfield spent the rest of the day around the big ranch. Riders came and went and there was bustling work — baking, and leather being tanned, blacksmith jobs and other tasks. In the afternoon a girl came out on a side veranda and Corky Ellsworth at once went to her. She came down the step and took Ellsworth's arm.

The Ranger studied her slim loveliness as she walked with Ellsworth toward the tall visitor. Her big brown eyes smiled up at Hatfield as he bowed and touched his Stetson brim. She had rich dark hair and all the other appurtenances of real beauty.

"This is Jim Hays that I told yuh of, Lucia," said Ellsworth. "He saved my life in town."

"I am very grateful," she said.

Hatfield chatted with Lucia for a time. Her musical voice and charm were such that the Ranger could well understand the fascination she had for Corky Ellsworth, so great as to cause him to volunteer to throw in his lot with the Mace. It would have taken a much less acute observer than Hatfield to see that the two were in love.

The officer had found out all he could at the ranch. He waited until after dark to start his trip back to Mullen City since he did not wish to be seen coming from the direction of the Mace by Potter or the lawyer's agents. He ate supper at the ranch and, promising to return soon, moved on the sorrel toward the river.

Late that night he crossed the stream well to the south of Mullen City and swung the golden sorrel toward the settlement. He had a good deal to turn over in his analytical mind. He had met the Criles and some of the big ranch's opponents. There was a definite connection between counselor Potter and the band of vicious outlaws under Joe the Knife. Potter obviously desired the destruction of the Mace and of Colonel Madison Crile. But where did the missing citizens from the east bank come into the picture?

Lights were on in town when he reached the outskirts, and he could hear the music from the Palace. Saddled mustangs stood in the gutter, reins over the rail, waiting for their owners to finish drinking in the saloons.

He slowed his horse, for he knew that he must be wary. There was always the chance that he had been recognized during his operations against Potter and Joe the Knife. They might be watching for him and a hidden marksman could put a bullet through his back without the slightest warning.

The Ranger circled around the back roads and came to a side way into town north of the Palace. He dropped his reins and went quickly along the walk under the wooden awnings, reaching the big saloon and hotel without incident.

There was music in the annex, but few dancers. The bar was crowded and he glanced over the batwings and saw that bunches of men were standing around, listening to what this one or that one had to say. They looked troubled and they looked angry.

Potter had a table in a corner, a favored position, and was enjoying a late supper with a bottle to wash it down. Another pretty dancehall girl sat with him. George Loese was very much in evidence. He was holding forth to the gathering.

When the tall man entered, stopping just inside the door for a moment, Loese paused and looked up quickly to see who it was. Loese recognized Hatfield and gave him a friendly wave, beckoning him forward.

"And here's an hombre right now can tell yuh how the Mace guns folks who set foot on their range!" cried Loese, indicating Hatfield. "He was over there the other day and

they opened fire on him without warnin'!
Ain't it so?"

CHAPTER VIII
MISSING

Every eye was turned on the Ranger. While Hatfield could hold his own in any company, this public attention was none too welcome at the moment. Instantly, though, his quick brain sought a way to make use of the enforced limelight.

"That's right," he replied boldly, moving toward the counter and joining the crowd. "I was mindin' my own business and bullets begun whistlin' over me. It was that old goat of a colonel and his boys gunnin' me. I'd be dead if I didn't have a mighty fast hoss under me."

Loese was highly gratified, and Potter was all ears as he heard the big fellow speak against the Criles.

Hatfield called for a drink and listened as Loese went on talking.

"I tell yuh, we got to wipe out the Criles and smash the Mace!" insisted Loese. "This is the sixth man who's dropped out of sight

89

like he'd been spirited away, just because he set foot on Crile's range."

"The Mace done killed another hombre?" asked the Ranger.

"Yes suh." A heavy-set man in rancher clothing who stood next to Loese nodded. "My brother Ed is missin', since early this mornin'. Loese and two other fellers saw him cross the river to catch a strayed mustang. He ain't been seen since. We went over and hunted but lost the trail."

"Yuh got every right to hit the Mace, Brophy," said Loese earnestly. "Yuh'll never see yore brother again."

Without volition a chill touched the Ranger. Another man had evaporated into thin air!

He waited and listened, and soon had the story. He learned that Mike Brophy whose brother was missing, was a small rancher whose spread lay northeast of Mullen City. The brother, Ed, had owned property above that which had belonged to Rob Davis, another supposed victim of the Mace.

"Wonder if there's a quit-claim deed to this Ed Brophy's property in Potter's files," mused Hatfield, listening carefully.

He soon learned that one of the two other witnesses to Ed Brophy's disappearance was present in the saloon now. Hatfield recognized him. He had seen that bearded face, and knew the man was a close crony of Loese's. He did not doubt that the third witness would turn out to be another of the counselor's close adherents.

The pattern was beginning to grow clearer to Hatfield. He had realized, as soon as he heard of Ed Brophy's loss, why Joe the Knife and his gang had come to Potter's office. They had reported to carry out a task for the counselor and Hatfield would have been willing to swear without further evidence that Joe the Knife and his men had picked off Ed Brophy and carried him away with them. Potter, through Loese, was blaming it on the Mace.

He studied Mike Brophy, the rancher whose brother had been lost. Brophy was a sturdy man of about forty. He had a sober face and good features, with honest blue eyes and a firm jaw. He looked like a strong character, the sort of man who could be depended on in a pinch. He did not have too much to say, but when he did speak others listened with deference.

Mike Brophy was a natural leader of men, once he had made up his mind, and he looked the part. His leather pants and half-boots, his blue shirt and clean bandanna were not flashy, but expressed his plain good sense. He wore a flat-topped "Nebraska" hat and in his cartridge belt rode a Colt's revolver of large caliber.

Hatfield was interested in Mike Brophy, because he was hunting someone who was fitted to represent the honest people around Mullen City. Everybody seemed to know and look up to this rancher.

"I was a friend of Crile's," Brophy said slowly and weightily. "Up to a few weeks ago I'd have called any man a liar who said the Mace would kill folks on their range. But I'm shore beginnin' to boil over. Pore Ed!"

His grief was deep for, from past experience, he had reason to believe he would never see his brother again.

"How long you people goin' to stand for it, is what gets me!" cried Loese. "Why don't yuh band together? Get every gun in Mullen City and roundabout and go down there and wipe out Crile!"

It was strong talk but there were many men willing to listen.

"Who savvies which one of yuh will be next?" prodded Loese. "If a hoss or cow crosses the river, yuh don't dare go after it."

From the sullen looks and the growls of hate, Hatfield knew that a mass battle must be shaping up. Given a little more time, and all the men on this side of the river would unite against the Mace. Yet Crile had many hard-riding, fast-shooting *vaqueros* and cowboys. It would not be an easy victory. But it would be a bloody battle.

"Next I got to try and rope Potter," decided the Ranger.

He must learn more details, find just what it was that the counselor was after. It must be more than simple revenge against Colonel Crile, for such a man as Potter craved wealth and power above everything else.

Already the Ranger had established a bond between Loese, who was Potter's creature, and himself. He thought it over and, forming a plan, left the Palace ahead of Loese. He went to the next corner, aware that Loese lived somewhere close to Potter's home, and waited.

It was over an hour before Loese came out of the saloon and walked slowly up the street. Hatfield leaned against the wall, turned away from Loese. Loese came up behind him and slapped him on the back.

"What's up, hombre?"

Hatfield could draw with the speed of legerdemain, and he made one of his fastest whirls. The heavy Colt snapped from the oiled holster into the slim hand and the hammer spur was back under his thumb, the muzzle aimed straight at Loese's vitals before the small man could make a move or even open his mouth to gasp his alarm.

Loese was as good as dead if Hatfield raised his thumb and Loese knew it only too well. The black muzzle of the pistol made chills run up and down the little man's spine.

"Don't!" he whimpered.

"Oh, it's you, George! Sorry." Hatfield flipped his gun back into its holster and grinned.

"Phew! Yuh had me worried!" Loese was shaking like a leaf. He pulled himself together. "Yuh're mighty touchy, feller."

"Never come up behind me like that," warned Hatfield. "Yuh're a friend, but I'm sort of jumpy these days."

The hint was enough for Loese. The Ranger's panther speed and obvious ability had helped complete Loese's estimation of the tall stranger in Mullen City. Anyone who would pull a gun just because someone touched his shoulder must be on the dodge.

"I never see anyone as fast as you on the draw," complimented Loese. "Let's go over to Pete's and have a snifter. It's quiet there and we can pow-wow in the back room."

Pete's was past Potter's office, a small place run by a Mexican. There were only a few drinkers in the front room. Loese led his tall friend to a private room in the rear and a Mexican youth in a dirty white apron brought them *tequila.*

"I reckon yuh're on the run," said Loese, sizing Hatfield up with what the small man considered a keen look. Loese took pride in his supposed acumen. "Don't be scared. I'm yore pard. And yuh needn't be worried in this town. Potter's the best lawyer in Texas and he could get anybody off."

"I heard of the counselor." Hatfield nodded. "That's one reason I drifted this way, Loese."

"It's plain they're after yuh. I ain't askin' questions but I'd like to give yuh a tip. Talk to Potter. He'll help yuh."

"S'pose they got a warrant for yuh and a dozen witnesses against yuh?"

Loese laughed and sipped his *tequila.* Hatfield had assumed a nervous mien, and Loese was enjoying his mental superiority over his worried companion.

"Think nothin' of it. Potter can fix anything."

"Mebbe I'll go talk to him in the mornin'."

"I'll put in a word for yuh." Loese was patronizing. "What's yore handle, anyway? At least what yuh go by?"

Hatfield hesitated, then replied, "Jim Hays."

"Good enough."

When the Ranger left Loese, he took care of Goldy, then retired to his room in the Palace. He had worked it so that he had a recommendation of sorts to Potter and he intended to make the best use he could of it.

He slept late. After he had washed up he breakfasted leisurely at the Texas Lunch, so it was nearly ten o'clock when the Ranger ducked in the front door of Potter's office.

Potter sat at his desk in the rear, his broad back to the wall. There was a ruby tinge on the end of his nose and he kicked a drawer shut with his foot, a bottle and glass clanking together. Potter had just been enjoying a morning eye-opener, a "mist-dispeller."

He cleared his throat and frowned. He was a flamboyant figure this morning in a light-blue jacket, white stock and fancy ruffled shirt. His trousers were fawn color and fitted to his well-shaped legs. On his face was a self-important expression as he stared at Hatfield, smoothing his brown hair which had been freshly brushed and sleeked with pomade.

"What can I do for you, sir?" he demanded

briskly, folding his hands before him on the desk.

"My name's Hays, Counselor Potter. I was talkin' with George Loese and he said I ought to see yuh."

By Potter's look and manner the Ranger knew that Loese had told Potter about the prospective client.

"Yes? What's your trouble?"

Potter waved a graceful hand toward a chair opposite him and Hatfield sat down. He was aware of the lawyer's steady, searching eyes, but he had his story all prepared.

"S'pose there was a warrant out for a feller and a deputy on his trail," he said, with the proper amount of hesitancy. "And if somehow this sheriff caught up and took same hombre prisoner. He'd be in the calaboose. Could you get him out?"

A small smile loosened the lawyers lips.

"My friend, there's no sense in beatin' about the bush. I take it you're on the dodge. What reason have you to think you're important enough for a community to send a special officer after you?"

"I know they have," replied Hatfield earnestly. "I seen him twice and just got out ahead of him and the local law he called on. And last week I met a pard who told me they'd took up a collection out there just so's I could be brought back."

Potter whistled. "You must have done it up brown. What county is it?"

Hatfield again allowed the right moment of hesitation before replying, "Well, Crockett."

"That's all the way over to the Pecos. How many men did you kill?"

"Six, all told. I only meant to down a couple when I held up the store but they kept comin' and by the time I got out they was all lyin' stretched on the floor. Wasn't my fault."

"No, I can see that," murmured the counselor. In a louder voice he asked, "Who told you to come to me?"

"This pard I mentioned. Name of Mex. He operated down on the Border around Brownsville. He used to be a pal of Joe the Knife."

Potter's sharp look did not catch the Ranger unawares. Hatfield never changed his manner.

"You're acquainted with Joe?" asked Potter.

"No, I ain't had the pleasure. Heard tell of him, though, and how you got him off down there. It was mighty slick."

Potter seemed satisfied. He nodded.

"You keep in touch with Loese, understand?" he said. "I'll guarantee they won't hold you even if you're arrested."

Potter considered the big man before him, rested his left elbow against his side and, head bent, tapped his cheek with his fingertips. Hatfield had seen Potter's gesture before, and realized it must be a habit the man had acquired when turning over a point in his sharp mind.

"Loese says you're the fastest man with a gun he's ever seen," Potter said suddenly. Apparently he had reached his conclusion. "How would you like to feel really safe and at the same time earn a little money?"

"It sounds like just what the sawbones ordered, Counselor."

"Hang around. Loese will tell you about it. We'll find some work for you before long."

Hatfield took his leave. Potter asked no fee from him, which was unusual, for such attorneys who catered to outlaws demanded their money in advance as a rule.

The Ranger stayed in town, and the day passed uneventfully. He drank that evening with George Loese, who seemed to have accepted him as a full-fledged comrade. Then he rested up, waiting for the call he was sure would come from the lawyer.

It was the following night when George Loese led the officer through a back road to

Potter's stable. Here were several men who had just come in. Their saddled mustangs stood in the shadows. A bony breed, a Texican, stepped forward, towering over Loese and about eye to eye with the mighty Ranger. However the thin man was not nearly so powerfully built as Hatfield.

"Howdy, George," the breed said. "We had to come in for liquor and food. What's new?"

"I got a recruit for yuh, Joe," said Loese. "The chief says he's all right. Let's step inside the barn for a minute."

They could talk in the stable without being observed from outside. Loese lighted a lantern and Joe the Knife sized up the aspiring member of the outlaw band.

"Meet Jim Hays," drawled Loese. "He savvies a pard of yores, Joe."

"Yeah? Who's that?" The Knife was not particularly suspicious, but inquired out of curiosity.

"Mex," said Hatfield. "That's what we used to call him. He operated back and forth across the Border not far from Brownsville."

"Yuh mean Mex Vasquez?" the Knife asked helpfully.

"I reckon that was it." Hatfield knew there were hundreds of "Mex's" just as there were

"Tex's," and had felt safe enough in venturing the nickname.

"A good hombre."

Joe the Knife nodded, seeming to be satisfied.

Chapter IX
Graveyard Depot

Hatfield was introduced to half a dozen toughs who had come with the Knife, while Joe himself slipped to Potter's back door to confer with the chief. The Ranger wondered if they would pick up a victim on their way out of town.

Evidently it was as Joe the Knife had said, however. They had run short of whisky. For when they rode out of Mullen City a couple of hours later they carried a supply of liquor and some provisions with them.

And the tall Ranger on the golden sorrel rode with them, a recruit in the killer band of Joe the Knife!

Hatfield followed the Knife who was mounted on a ghost-gray mustang with long legs and a nervous but space-consuming stride. They crossed the river and picked up speed on rolling Mace range, under a chunk of moon.

It was plain enough to the Ranger that

they were headed for that mountainous region northwest of Crile's into which Harry Tate had plunged. Somewhere in that swale of woods and upheaved rocks these dangerous killers must have their camp. Its exact location would be a valuable piece of information to the law.

The outlaws would guard its site jealously though, for it meant their safety. If Joe the Knife and his followers ever suspected the tall recruit they would kill him on the spot without the slightest hesitation, and the Ranger was well aware of this. He believed he had worked his way into the good graces of Potter and hence into the band, but there was one possible danger he could not take any precautions against. Harry Tate was not with the small party which had come in that night with Joe the Knife.

There was a chance that Tate might have observed the man on the golden sorrel that day when the Mace had opened fire and pursued Hatfield. If Tate had had field glasses and had carefully watched the proceedings he would have seen Crile let Hatfield go free. And that might be enough of a slip to spell the Ranger's ruin!

Dawn was graying the sky behind them when they walked their horses up a narrow trail in the wooded fastnesses. Great black pines reared over them and because of the needle droppings of centuries they left few imprints. They had been moving on broken ground for over two hours, winding this way and that.

Joe the Knife reached a crest and they paused for breath. The trees hid the back trail and none of the range could be seen from this point. Ahead sharp boulders stuck from the earth. The country opened up and there was a small stream running in the dip.

The bony leader silently pushed on, slanting down the steep slope of the ravine. The hoofs slid in the slippery needles and reins were held tight to keep up the heads of the horses. They stopped to let the animals drink a little, then Joe the Knife crossed the swift-running brook and plunged into a thicket. Past this was a rock-strewn stretch which the mountain torrent had formed during freshets. No sign at all was left there for a tracker to follow.

There seemed to be no way out of the deep ravine, but half a mile farther a side cut offered a narrow gate. The grade was negotiable to horses and up it went Joe the Knife, his men after him. The light was good and there was red in the sky as the sun rose.

Over the ravine were more slopes, broken mountains rising higher, with pine woods and brush clothing their sides. The way led north a mile, then suddenly a sharp voice said:

"Howdy, boys!"

It was the voice of an outlaw guard watching the trail. He was sitting with his back to a big tree and hidden by it, a carbine in his hands.

The party replied to the sentinel's call and moved on. There was a slight rise to the left and more tangled brush. Joe the Knife stopped, dismounted, and the rest followed suit, Hatfield among them.

"Take the hosses to the corral," Joe ordered one of his men. "C'mon, Hays. Camp's this way."

High rock steps took them to the top of the rise and, breasting the screen of bushes, the Ranger saw the bandit hideout in a roughly circular hollow.

It was a perfect spot for a camp, protected from spying eyes and from winds that might sweep through. There were rocks which would break up smoke from the cook fires, and a crystal spring large enough to water horses and a hundred men. Overhanging ledges served with the aid of stretched tarpaulins to protect food and other equipment, such as ammunition.

Joe the Knife led the way in. A bearded

outlaw squatted near a fire over which a battered coffee pot simmered.

"Let's have some chow, Fred," ordered the bony leader.

In the morning light the breed's white knife scar stood out on his brown cheek. His deep-set eyes glowed and he looked the part of an outlaw who had killed a Texas Ranger and got away with it — with the aid of the rascally lawyer whose deadly schemes he was now furthering.

" 'Mornin'," somebody called, and a bearded, sallow-faced man rose from his blanket bed, stretched, and came over to join the new arrivals.

It was Harry Tate. Potter had cleaned him up for the trial when he had depicted Tate as a mother's boy sadly put upon by the Mace, but now he was greasy and uncombed and rumpled. Food and tobacco had stained his shirt and his leather pants were old and scratched. On his hands was the grime of several days.

Hatfield squatted near the fire as the cook poured tin mugs of steaming coffee for the party. He watched Tate from the corner of his eye, for he must be ready to try to fight his way out if Tate roused Joe the Knife's suspicion. Tate's watery eyes rested on him for a moment, and the Ranger held his breath. But there was no sign of recognition in Tate's look. Instead he glanced inquiringly at Joe the Knife.

"Meet Jim Hays, Tate," said the Knife. "Recruit. Yuh show him around later. Reckon we'll all enjoy some shut-eye first."

"Howdy, Hays," said Tate. "Welcome to Buzzards' Roost."

Hatfield was relieved, for he had been almost certain Tate would have given some slight warning if he had observed the scene between the Ranger and the Criles. Hatfield believed he could thank his stars that Tate had not been carrying fieldglasses.

There were about three dozen outlaws at the hideout. They seemed to compose Joe the Knife's main force.

When Hatfield woke from his nap after noon, the air was warm, although the camp was shaded from the worst of the sunlight. Groups of toughs lounged around him, drinking from tin mugs filled with whisky, playing cards or mumblety-peg, anything to while away the time.

The cook had dinner ready. Big steaks carved from a side of beef, no doubt one of Crile's animals stolen from the lower range, had been broiled on sharpened sticks. There was hardtack, and liquor to wash the food down.

The Ranger rose and stretched himself. He rolled a quirly and made no attempt to wash up at the spring, for a coating of dirt and whiskers would be the usual thing here. Harry Tate got up from a group and came to him. Joe the Knife was still sleeping under a ledge. Curious eyes sized up the tall bandit recruit.

"Yuh must be hungry," said Tate, kindly enough. "Help yoreself. I'm just startin' to eat."

Tate nodded and the Ranger went over and filled a tin plate with meat and biscuits. He saw the coffee pot steaming and poured himself a cup of the liquid, spiking it with whisky so as not to appear different from the other outlaws. A small wooden keg of liquor sat propped on a flat rock, handy for tapping.

He joined Tate and sat down by the sallow man to eat.

"Yuh got a swell layout here, Tate," he commented.

"Yeah. We're safe as bugs," Tate answered.

Joe the Knife rolled over and yawned. He kicked off his blankets, got up, and went to have an eye-opener at the keg before dinner.

Time went slowly, with nothing much to do. Gambling and drinking were the only diversions at the camp although most of the men were wanted by the law and safety meant something until boredom drove them out. Late in the afternoon Hatfield spoke to Harry Tate.

"I'd like to see to my hoss. Is it all right to walk around some?"

"Shore. Why not?"

Tate went with him, showing him a faint path to the horse corrals. In natural dips below the depot the outlaws held about a hundred mustangs. Long pine boles had been cut and, secured horizontally, served to fill in gaps in the brush and rock fences. Goldy had been turned in here. The sorrel came to the Ranger who began to groom his horse after leading the gelding outside the pen.

The saddles hung on racks made from lengths of timber.

"Now yuh savvy the way, I'll go back to the game," said Tate, and left the recruit working on the golden sorrel.

For a while the Ranger was busy as he saw to Goldy. It was quiet down by the corrals and no one seemed to be watching him. Turning out the sorrel when he had finished, Hatfield went around the corrals to the far side. He thought there might be a back approach to the outlaw depot which would come in handy in case a future attack might be planned.

He came on a faint path winding through pine woods and his boots made only faint sounds on the soft needles as he walked on for a few hundred yards. Then the trail ended abruptly at a steep bank which led down into a great natural clearing. Big vultures wheeled up from the other side as he showed himself on the brink.

The light was good and Hatfield had a trained eye. Glancing back to make certain he was not being followed he slid down into the depression. All about him were colored resinous masses in stained rock matrices.

Hatfield had studied mining engineering for a time before joining the Texas Rangers, and knew considerable about rock formations. Curious now, he squatted before an outcropping to examine it more closely. Browns, yellows, blacks, and dirty white were visible. He could make out crystal formations with some streaks of silvery material. There were obvious signs of iron, common to most regions, and worthless in such small quantity.

"Galena in there, too," he muttered, "but it ain't anything to get excited about."

Something in the back of his busy mind was nagging at him. He rose to move on around the big arena in order to check on strange formations.

"Looks like this is just one surface out-croppin'," he decided. "Mebbe mountains of it around."

He thought back over what he had learned on the mystery of the Mace. And he recalled the night in Potter's office when he had been interrupted by Joe the Knife.

"That letter!" he murmured. "Must be it."

He had not had an opportunity to read in full the correspondence between Potter and the company in San Antonio.

Something else checked this train of thought as he studied the spot where the vultures had been at work. He could see where the gravel had been disturbed by the big birds, and suddenly a chill raced down his spine as he saw the stiffened arm of a man sticking out.

He picked up a sharp piece of rock and dug farther, enough to expose the torso. The dead man had on a leather jacket and on its breast Hatfield could make out initials in red yarn: E. B.

"Ed Brophy!" He knew he had found the end of the trail for Mike Brophy's brother. He pushed gravel back on the body and moved along the far side of the cut. There were several spots where the bank had been recently dug up and replaced.

Hatfield was sure now that he had solved the mystery of those who had disappeared on Mace range. He heard Harry Tate calling him and hurriedly retreated, for they might well resent his presence in the arena. But the mystery of the missing men was clearing up — fast!

Chapter X
Home Ranch

Corky Ellsworth whistled cheerily as he worked in the stable yard of the Mace home ranch that fine morning. The world seemed perfect to the young cowpuncher who had thrown in his lot with the Criles. Perfect for him, anyway, though he wished that the rest of Texas and particularly the neighbors around Mullen City would understand how splendid the Criles were.

A task to be done had kept Ellsworth from accompanying Jeff Crile to the southwest range. Jeff had ridden out with a score of Mace *vaqueros* and cowboys to handle the big herds of cattle down there. Ellsworth had promised to join them later in the day.

The great ranch basked in the hot sunshine. Mexican women chattered as they baked bread in big outdoor ovens or washed clothing at the wooden troughs supplied by pipes from upstream. There were horses and colts in the roomy corrals, and armed men about the Mace made for security.

For Colonel Crile dared not relax his guard. A military man and a shrewd judge of human nature, Madison Crile was well aware of the growing tension between his neighbors across the river and the Mace outfit. It had to snap sooner or later and according to Crile's idea it would not be long before the ranch must fight for its life.

Ellsworth had gathered this for himself or through Jeff, who confided in him. It would be a tough battle, according to the colonel. The Mace would be outnumbered and would be fighting not only shady opponents but misguided citizens who believed themselves in the right. Such citizens made much tougher opponents than hireling gunslingers.

But Ellsworth would stay with the Mace. Lucia Crile had become everything to him and thoughts of home, of his own plans, had quickly faded after he had come to the Mace and fallen under the spell of her sparkling eyes.

The Criles had taken him in and after a brief period of observation had agreed with Jeff that Corky Ellsworth was about as fine a young fellow as could be found in Texas. Strong and tall in his neat cowboy outfit, his easy-going nature and quick smile had won them all.

Ellsworth had been delayed, because Whitefoot had cast a shoe. The ranch blacksmith had replaced the missing one, and now Corky had just finished grooming his beautiful gelding. He turned to go to the rack and get his saddle. As he went around the corner of the stable he met Lucia, slimly girlish in riding clothes. Her rich dark hair was caught up under a Stetson and she carried a riding crop.

"Corky! Good morning!" As her brown eyes looked into his, her smile, he thought, would have melted a stone image.

"Lucia! Every day yuh're prettier!"

The compliment pleased her. "I saw you out here and thought you'd help me saddle my horse. I want to go for a ride."

She had many *vaqueros* only too happy to serve her but Ellsworth was flattered by the privilege. She followed him into the shed where hung her special saddle, a hand-carved, silver-inlaid Mexican job which her father had given her.

Ellsworth turned. Her red lips were so inviting he could not resist any longer. Swiftly he took her in his arms and kissed her.

"Lucia!" he whispered.

"Corky!"

The same old story was vitally fresh to them. It seemed to them that the world was filled with magic and that the sun would always shine.

"Yuh reckon yore dad will give his consent to our marryin'?" asked Ellsworth after a time.

She laughed. "Yes, but you must tell him. And I know Mother will be happy about it."

Colonel Crile came from the *hacienda*. Ellsworth was rather in awe of the grim owner of the Mace although Crile had treated him with the utmost courtesy and kindness. The young man looked up to Lucia's father as he might to any wiser, older leader, and besides the colonel was Lucia's parent.

"Ellsworth!" called Crile.

Ellsworth and Lucia went out into the yard, Corky carrying her saddle. Crile's keen glance touched them and Ellsworth had a guilty feeling as he wondered if the colonel knew he had just kissed his daughter.

"Yuh're goin' out, Lucia?" asked the colonel. "Be shore to take a guard with yuh, dear. Corky, I want to go down to the southwest pasture and see how Jeff's doin' with that big herd. Yuh ready?"

116

"Yes suh."

Ellsworth would have preferred to go with Lucia, who was a most skillful rider. She was as impatient of restraint as he was, and liked to skim along over the rolling range. He knew she would pick a mettled, skittish mount for herself.

While Colonel Crile was saddling a tall bay, Ellsworth, helped Lucia ready the mount she had chosen, a black gelding named Satan on account of his tricky nature. Satan liked to feign obedience, to pretend that he was a well-behaved, decent horse and when he had thrown his rider off guard, then Satan would show his real self. But Lucia often rode him.

Lucia rode with her father and Ellsworth for an hour as they moved over the fine Mace south range. But the steady pace did not please her. "I'm going back," she finally cried.

She laughed and whirled Satan, picking up speed and galloping at full-tilt away from them. Her horse tried to swerve and fight but the Spanish bit pulled him into line. She was as graceful as a bird in the saddle and turned to wave at them.

"Hadn't I better see her home, suh?" asked Corky.

"No, let her go," said Crile. "She's as wild

as a boy when she's in one of those moods, son. She has to ride." He shouted after Lucia: "Pick up two guards if yuh venture north of the ranch."

Lucia gave another flirt of her gloved hand as though she heard her father's order. She was traveling at breakneck speed. The two men turned away and moved on toward the spot where they would find Jeff and the men.

It was a golden opportunity and Ellsworth screwed up his courage. He was alone with Lucia's father, and this was the moment to speak up.

He stole a glance at the bearded cheek of Colonel Crile. The most intense pride mingled with stern acceptance of life's blows in the Mace chief's expression. The South had lost the war and this had been a bitter pill, but Crile had swallowed it. There had been personal tragedies, too — the loss of a child and other saddening experiences. Lately the growing hatred of the people around the big ranch had gnawed at Crile's soul.

"Colonel!" As he spoke, Ellsworth felt the utmost embarrassment, for he knew he had committed himself.

"Yes, my boy. What is it?" Crile's voice was kind, and Corky took heart.

"Suh, me and Lucia. I mean Lucia and
I." He broke off, and his bronzed cheeks
were flushed as Crile watched him. "Would
yuh object if I asked her, that is, what would
yuh say if I was to marry her."

It was out, and Ellsworth waited for an
outburst of temper. But Madison Crile gave
one of his rare smiles. He moved his horse
closer to Ellsworth and slapped the young
man on the back.

"If yuh have Lucia's consent yuh have
mine, Corky. Yuh've fitted right in here with
us and I would like nothin' better than to
have yuh for my son."

"Thanks." Relief flooded Ellsworth's heart
and his quick, infectious grin touched his
handsome face. "I was thinkin' it over and
figured if yuh agreed that it would be
mighty nice for Lucia and her mother not
to be too far apart, suh. I can sell out the
ranch I bought and come down this way."

"I'll give yuh as much range as yuh desire."

"I'd rather buy it, Colonel."

Crile understood a young man's pride and
he nodded.

"Whichever way suits yuh, son. I appreci-
ate yore fine consideration of Lucia's mother
and me."

It was all settled and Ellsworth rode on,

his spirit dancing on air.

They found Jeff Crile and the cowboys later and joined them. It was after six o'clock when they all returned to the home ranch and, tired from the day's work, began to unsaddle.

A *vaquero* carrying a carbine approached Colonel Crile.

"Senor Crile, the senora weesh to know where ees Senorita Lucia. She come weeth you?"

Corky Ellsworth heard the question, and it was his first premonition of disaster. He turned cold as ice, and he saw that Crile was instantly alarmed.

The colonel swore hotly. "She's here, isn't she? Didn't she get home? Come, speak up!"

"No, senor. We do not see her since she ride weeth you."

"That cussed Satan!" said Ellsworth. "I begged her not to take him."

Big Jeff Crile hurried over. "What's wrong?"

"Lucia's missin'," replied Ellsworth. "She's been gone since before noon!"

"Saddle up!" shouted Colonel Crile. "Follow me!"

Satan had not returned to the ranch as he

might have done had he succeeded in throwing his rider.

The Mace outfit was quickly on the way, spreading out to pick up Satan's trail. The men cast about after cutting what they were sure was the sign of Lucia's horse. It ran west of the ranch as she had skirted around the buildings that way and gone on north for a time at full-tilt.

By this time the sun was almost gone, and the darkness near. Sweat stood out cold on Corky Ellsworth's brow in spite of the heat in the air. The armed might of the Mace behind him, Colonel Crile pushed on, the worst of forebodings graying his features.

Now as the night was upon them, a keen-eyed Mace rider sang out and pointed. There was a dark speck ahead, over the next faint rise.

They reached it as darkness fell. It was Satan, a bullet-hole through his brain. They got down to study the find and discovered that the horse had broken a leg.

"Sis carried a gun, of small caliber," growled Jeff Crile. "Looks like she shot him after he went down in that crusted hole a little ways back."

Crile had brought lanterns and they searched for Lucia's footprints. They found her trail in softer spots and it led at an angle in the direction of the home ranch. They had gone about a mile from the spot where they had come on Satan's carcass when they cut the sign of half a dozen shoed mustangs traveling in a bunch.

"Ridden hosses!" announced young Ellsworth as they read the traces by the light of the lanterns.

"There was a fight here!" snapped Jeff Crile. "Look! Here's her revolver." From the sand Jeff picked up a small pistol. The shells in the cylinders had been fired.

There were no more footprints. The horses of the party which had met Lucia had circled and turned back northwest.

It was slow moving in the night for the trail had to be checked every few minutes, but the silent party pushed on. Every man knew that Lucia had fallen into the hands of the outlaw band which hid in the fastnesses of the mountains ahead, and every man's heart was heavy burdened.

CHAPTER XI
BREAK

Jim Hatfield came awake suddenly, all his faculties alert. He was rolled in his blanket under the rock shelf of the cliff protecting the bandit hideout.

The cook fire had died down, so there was but a faint glow in the immediate vicinity of the coals, but there was enough moonlight for him to make out the shape of things. The Ranger congratulated himself on his success in getting into the outlaws' haven, where he had been storing away information and piecing together vital facts he needed if he hoped to smash Frank Potter and his array of gunslingers.

There were outlaws sleeping near him. The Ranger had been on a hair-trigger and a single sound had promptly awakened him. The approach of a party to the camp had brought him instantly to his senses.

He waited, watching from under veiling lashes as he lay on his back. It was not unusual for two or three of the killers to slip in after dark, for Hatfield had learned that Joe the Knife kept spies and scouting parties observing the Mace.

"Joe, Joe!" called the excited voice of one of the approaching men. He hurried past the fire, hailing the outlaw boss.

"What's the matter — you drunk?" growled Joe the Knife, roused from his slumber. He sat up, swearing at being disturbed.

"No, I ain't drunk! Wait till yuh hear what we done!"

A trail-stained, bearded outlaw appeared close to the fire as Joe the Knife's bony figure stepped forth. Others were sitting up around camp now, and from habit reached for their guns.

"What did yuh do, then?" demanded Joe.

"We were hidin' in a grove a few miles north of the Mace home ranch when we sighted a rider," explained the bearded fellow. "Danged if it wasn't that Crile girl ridin' our way! She was on a mighty fast hoss and we just waited, but then her mustang steps in a hole and throws her. She had to shoot the critter and we hustled down and picked her up. The little devil fought like a wildcat. Emptied her pistol at us and she grooved Vern, but it was only a flesh bite."

"Yuh mean yuh captured Lucia Crile?" cried Joe the Knife.

"Yes, suh. Here they come now, fetchin' her in."

"Well, fry my hide!" Joe the Knife was stunned. "Look here, Lenny, s'pose the Mace outfit picks up yore trail and follers yuh here? They'll be as roused as a hornets' nest at this."

"No, they'll never track us," insisted Lenny. "We come way around west and doubled back on the rocks and through the creek. That's why we're so late gettin' in."

Several more outlaws came over the rim into the hideout and before them walked the proud figure of Lucia Crile. Hatfield was as stunned as was Joe the Knife, but for a different reason. It was a major blow in his fight against Potter's outlaw empire that Lucia should have been captured. Now he must sacrifice every advantage he had gained, and even his life if necessary, in an attempt to save her.

As Joe the Knife realized the importance of the prisoner the bony killer grew excited. He kicked some dry branches on the coals and the fire blazed up, lighting the scene.

"Wait till Potter hears this!" gloated the Knife. "It will bust up the Mace. We'll needle the cusses into a suicide attack. Nice work, Lenny. What a hostage we got!"

Lucia moved across the rough ground toward the fire. She stopped and looked up at Joe the Knife. She was white with anger, and weary from the long ride.

"Are you the leader here?" she demanded. If she feared him she was hiding it beneath her pride.

"Yes, ma'am, I reckon I am." The Knife grinned.

"Then you must give me a horse and let me go. You men have no right to hold me."

"Don't worry. We ain't goin' to harm one hair of yore pretty head, Senorita Crile." Joe the Knife made a sweeping bow. "Yuh're too valuable alive. Just settle down and behave yoreself and yuh'll be took care of."

Lucia's temper flared. "My father is Colonel Crile of the Mace! He'll never rest till you're punished for this. I warn you!"

"I savvy just who yore dad is," drawled Joe the Knife. "Say, yuh're mighty good lookin', ain't yuh?"

Hatfield stayed back in the shadow. A chance word surprised from Lucia if she recognized him, remembering him from that one visit to her father, as Deputy Sheriff Jim Hays, could mean his instant death. Worse, it could mean the loss of any forlorn hope that he might snatch her from the bandit stronghold.

Joe the Knife ordered water and food brought for the prisoner. After first refusing, Lucia sensibly accepted, taking a drink and eating a plate of stew warmed over from dinner.

"Dave, you rig a tarpaulin at the upper end of camp where that red cliff juts out," commanded Joe the Knife. "Fix up a bed of pine boughs and blankets for the lady. We'll make yuh comfortable, ma'am."

Soon Lucia was escorted to her quarters. Canvas rigged as a tent shielded her. Joe the Knife gave more orders.

"You drunken fools keep yore paws off her, savvy? I'll drill the first man who looks cross-eyed at her. I want a day and night guard to watch her but don't bother her. See she's fed."

"Where you bound, Joe?" asked Harry Tate.

The bony chief stretched as he stood up.

"I'm goin' right over and tell the boss what we got. It may make a big difference in his plans. We could catch the Mace off guard for shore. I'll bet they'll all be out huntin' the girl for days. We could even get in there and bust up the whole ranch."

Hatfield waited, close at hand. He knew he would have to wait before he could make any move toward rescuing Lucia. For while the fire burned high he would have no chance to go near the tarpaulin screen. He would have to hope and pray for his opportunity.

The Ranger well knew that bloody war was about to break in all its fury over the Mace. Not only would Potter and his outlaw allies be involved against the Crile faction, but Potter had worked up enmity between the decent elements east of the river, such men as Mike Brophy and his friends, and the Mace. He must, of course, do all he could to prevent that, but first of all he must save Lucia. He listened with foreboding to what the elated outlaws were saying.

"Yes, suh, the Criles are easy meat for us," boasted Joe the Knife. "This cinches it, Tate. We'll sick Brophy and his crew on 'em and when the Mace is about crushed we'll step in fresh and strong and wipe 'em out!"

It was good outlaw strategy. Hatfield knew that, and sensed the reasons. The hireling gunslingers Joe the Knife could command were none too effective against determined fighters such as Crile and his cowboys. But Brophy and his friends would match the Mace outfit. When both sides were ex-

128

hausted the bandits would clean up, and make good their boast.

"A thousand to one Mike Brophy is marked for a slug once he's carried out Potter's ideas," thought the Ranger.

It was hard not to grow rattled in the face of the looming juggernaut. Potter was winning, and events were shaping up to hurry his triumph. Even hick was on his side, or rather the bad luck of the Criles was responsible for tonight's coup. Hatfield's cool brain clicked as he figured his chances.

"I'll leave you in charge, Tate," he heard Joe the Knife say. "I'll make a flyin' run to Mullen and tip off the boss. Roy, Sam and Dick, you ride with me. Come on, we'll start right away."

Men were moving around in the camp and Hatfield edged off from the firelight as Joe the Knife and his three aides made ready to go after horses and saddle up. Hatfield hurried off, and reached the path to the corrals ahead of Joe the Knife.

"Take me along, Joe!" he begged the leader. "I'm tired of hangin' around camp."

"No, you stick here," commanded the Knife. "Yuh got to learn to obey orders in this outfit, Hays. We'll soon be back and I promise yuh'll see plenty action in the next few days. *Adios.*"

Hatfield glanced back. Harry Tate stood by the fire, looking at the stretched tarpaulin which hid Lucia Crile. Outside this a bandit sentry had taken up his post, a carbine across his knees as he sat on a flat rock.

Joe the Knife and his three cronies went through the brush screen and descended the rock steps, headed for the corrals. The rest of the men at the hideout grouped around Tate, talking over the exciting capture. Hatfield was in the darkness away from the fire, the rise casting a shadow over his tall figure. He went quietly through the bushes and out of sight of the outlaws, waited until he heard Joe the Knife and his guards riding past on the out-trail.

"I got about three hours to get goin'," the Ranger figured. "Then it will be daylight."

He hoped against hope that Tate and the others would go back to their blankets. Meanwhile he had a task to do, and he slipped down the path toward the corrals.

It was easy to call Goldy, for the beautiful sorrel had scented him and came at a soft whistle. He saddled his powerful gelding and, leaving Goldy outside the rail, went in to catch another mount. He wanted a fast one, for it would be a close race.

Other considerations were thrust into the back of his mind as he concentrated all his energy and thought on saving Lucia. By the next night it would be too late, for Joe the Knife would be back with Potter's orders. The issue between the Brophy faction and the Criles might even have been forced by then.

There was little light by which to pick a horse. Bunches of mustangs, many of them skittish and hostile toward a man afoot, stood in the pens. Hatfield had a rope halter he had appropriated from among the gear in the nearby racks.

A tall shape attracted him and he spoke in a gentling, low voice to the animal. It moved away at first but soon he was stroking its neck. He could feel the mustang quivering and knew he had caught a mettled creature. His caressing hand and soothing tone held the dark gelding as the Ranger felt over the horse.

He seemed to be sound. His breathing was good but whether he could stand a long run or not, must be left to chance. However, the bandits were good judges of horseflesh and the ones they stole were usually fine ones.

Hatfield set the halter and the dark gelding went out of the corral with him. He had a little trouble saddling up for the horse hated the cinches and bucked.

"Easy, easy," said the Ranger gently.

He put a foot in the stirrup and mounted. The gelding gave a few pitches, then stood quiet.

"Bueno," murmured Hatfield. "I'll have to trust yuh."

The walk which Hatfield had taken when he had discovered the burial place of Potter's victims was not the only stroll he had managed to take in the vicinity of the camp. He had been all around the hideout and knew the approaches.

He left Goldy and the dark horse standing with dropped reins under tall pines west of the corrals and, with his lariat on his shoulder, started up the slope toward the rock rim of the camp. By careful climbing he finally reached a spot from which he was able to look over the scene. The fire had burned down and most of the men had gone back to their blankets. Tate was about to turn in. The guard posted outside Lucia's shelter sat huddled on his rock, his back to the Ranger.

It was a steep descent and Hatfield fastened one end of his rope to the thick bole of a stunted cedar. By the aid of the lariat he began working down, praying his foot might not loosen any chunks of stone to alarm the killers. The bulge of the cliff helped hide him and he counted as well on the hung canvas.

"I hope she's sleepin'," he thought. "If she yells I'm a goner."

At the bottom he was among fallen boulders and in shadows black as ink. The tarpaulin was only a few feet from him. He waited, listening for sounds of Lucia.

Inch by inch the Ranger worked across the rocks closer to where the girl lay. He paused at a point he knew must be only arm's length from her. He must take a chance and let her know who was approaching.

"Lucia!" he whispered. "Quiet!"

He heard her give a startled gasp and she moved, starting a stone clacking as loud as a shot in the Ranger's ears.

"Who's there?" she asked, her voice low.

But the sentry had caught the noise of the stone. The outlaw stood up and stared at the tarpaulin wall.

"What's the matter, ma'am?" he inquired. "Yuh want somethin'?"

Hatfield flattened himself and did not move a muscle. Lucia did not answer for a moment, and the bandit shifted. Then the girl said softly:

"I'm all right, thank you."

The Ranger waited until the sentinel settled down again. The man rolled a quirly and lighted up, and the Ranger scented the burning tobacco. Tate and the others had quieted in their blankets but he must dispose of this guard, for Lucia could hardly move without the armed outlaw hearing her.

It took fifteen minutes for Hatfield to cover the few yards between the sentry and the rocks. He could not afford any mistake as he lunged and seized the bandit's throat, cutting off any outcry. His knee rammed into the small of the man's back and there was a brief tussle before the outlaw went limp.

Hatfield quickly took the guard's place on the flat rock and waited to see if Tate or any of the others had been disturbed. After a minute he breathed with relief, for there was no alarm. If Lucia heard the quick contest she did not make any outcry. Hatfield tried again:

"Lucia! Quiet! I'm goin' to take yuh home. It's Jim Hays."

"I hear you!" she whispered. "I'm ready." There was suppressed joy and excitement in her voice.

"Do just as I tell yuh," warned the Ranger. "I'm alone."

They must be very quiet, and yet he dared not linger long for there were over a score of brutal killers close at hand.

134

Lucia stood just inside the tarpaulin, waiting for him. He held out a hand and she seized it. She was trembling but she had courage and he led her toward where the lariat end hung down. The strong arms of the Ranger lifted her and she gripped the rope. By this she was able to reach the top of the rim. Hatfield swarmed up after her.

"I got hosses below," he whispered.

She could see his tall figure in the faint moonlight as they left the brush screen around the hideout and crossed toward the woods. He held her hand to guide her and prevent her from stumbling.

"Do you think we'll make it?" she asked anxiously.

"Shore we'll make it. Put everything yuh got into escapin', ma'am."

They were not yet out of danger by any means. If Tate and his gunslingers rushed out they could shoot down the man and recapture the woman.

CHAPTER XII
A RIDE FOR LIFE

Break of the new day framed Jim Hatfield
on the golden sorrel and beside him Lucia
Crile as she rode the dark gelding. The
horse which the Ranger had picked from
the outlaw corral had held the pace well.
The sun was coming up now, gilding the
wilderness.

They were still in rough terrain. Hatfield
had had only a general idea of the wooded
hills which occupied the north and northwest sections of the Mace. Outside of the
run when Joe the Knife had taken him to
the hideout he knew nothing of the mountains. As for Lucia she had visually confined
her riding to the open range for she liked
speed, but she had been able to give some
advice on the faint, winding paths they had
followed among the rocks.

The girl's face was pale and drawn. Her
clothes were stained with clay and earth.
But she smiled at the rugged Ranger as he

glanced at her.

"You needn't worry," she told him. "I won't faint."

"*Bueno.* Yuh're a brave girl."

She studied his grim face, the jaw drawn in by the tight chinstrap of his Stetson. He was a mighty figure and on his shirtfront now blazed the silver star on silver circle, emblem of the Texas Rangers.

"So my father's message reached the Rangers and you came to help us," said Lucia.

"Yes ma'am. I like to have a look-see at things before I open up, though. That's why I kept it to myself."

Lucia nodded. "That's a wise course, I think. It made it possible for you to get into the bandit camp. And if you hadn't been there, what would have happened to me?" Her admiration for him was boundless since he had brought her out of Joe the Knife's hideout. "I can't tell you how grateful I am!"

"Forget it, ma'am. Keep ridin'. We ain't out of the woods yet."

He knew that by this time Harry Tate would have discovered their absence and would be on their trail. And he kept glancing eastward in case Joe the Knife might loom up, returning from Mullen City.

It was slow going in spots where rocks and

uphill broke the trail. Now and then it was necessary to dismount and walk, leading the horses. The sun had risen and become a yellow disc when the Ranger and the girl pushed down a final wooded slope and saw before them the open range of the Mace.

"Now we can really make time!" cried Lucia.

Something shrieked through the air and the Ranger heard the light crack of a gun echo behind them. He turned in his saddle and saw Harry Tate and several of his erstwhile companions from the outlaw camp push up to the crest of the hill, hot after them.

"Ride!" he commanded, dropping back, so he could offer Lucia all possible protection.

She cut through the last of the rocks and trees, jumping her mount over a fallen pine. The sorrel came on after the dark gelding. On their right a long ridge petered out with a grove below it.

They hit the open country and picked up speed, gaining on Tate and his men. The sun glinted on the Ranger star as Hatfield watched back over a hunched shoulder to see how his foes were riding. Tate was in the van, spurring and quirting his mustang.

A hoarse shout from the west forced

Hatfield's attention that way. Riders were pouring from behind the grove and would cut off the girl and the Ranger before they could pass. It was a serious situation, and Hatfield called to Lucia, who was galloping on at a reckless pace.

She turned — and rode straight toward the new band! And then Hatfield recognized some of the horsemen. They were Mace riders, led by Colonel Crile, Jeff and Corky Ellsworth. At sight of Lucia they began to cheer, the *vaqueros* throwing their hats high in the air and driving toward the tall officer and the girl.

Tate and his bandit aides stopped in sliding spurts of dust, whirled and pelted back to the woods. There were at least twenty Mace fighters in view and Tate quit the chase at once, hunting escape. Crile waved an arm and a bunch of cowboys raced north around the grove after Tate.

The first to reach Lucia was Corky Ellsworth. He threw his arms around her and kissed her.

"Lucia! Are yuh hurt?"

"No, Corky. I'm fine. He brought me out." She indicated the Ranger.

Colonel Crile and Jeff tore up with some of the Mace waddies. Their horses were covered with dried lather, burs and other stickers and the men looked wan, showing how long they had been in the saddle.

Hatfield gave the Criles a few minutes in which to greet Lucia and hear her quick explanation. Then he said:

"Colonel, we better have a pow-wow. Let's start for yore ranch."

"Yes, Ranger."

Crile had fresh respect in his voice for he had recognized that silver star on silver circle and knew just what the big rider was. Even without this badge Hatfield would have been obeyed without question by the Mace chief for it was the tall man who had saved Lucia.

A couple of *vaqueros* were coming from the woods, having quit the chase after Tate and his men. Crile raised a silver whistle to his lips and blew shrill blasts on it.

A Mace cowboy reported. "They split up. Our hosses are wore out, boss."

Crile nodded. "We've been ridin' since yesterday without hardly a break, Ranger. Our animals are done in. Never catch up with a cart hoss now. Jeff, hang back and bring the rest of the boys home with yuh."

Ellsworth could not tear himself from Lucia's side. Hatfield signaled Colonel Crile and the two rode together, as the Mace cowboys strung out behind.

"We tried to follow the trail all night," explained Crile, glancing at the rugged face of the officer. "It led west and finally we lost it and had to give up entirely. We were mighty downhearted just before we sighted yuh, suh."

"McDowell had yore letter, Colonel. He sent me over. Now I've got the straight of the matter and I'm ready to fight. Are you?"

"I've been ready all along, Ranger. Yuh have only to command." All reservations had left Crile's mind as to the tall man who had come to the troubled Mace.

"My real handle is Hatfield, Jim Hatfield. There's a good deal to this business that I don't s'pose even you have been able to guess. I managed to dig a lot of it out by spyin' on Potter and Joe the Knife's bunch. The danger's still with us, Colonel Crile. As soon as yore enemy Potter finds that I pulled Lucia from the outlaw hideout, it will stampede him. He'll savvy he must win pronto or not at all."

"Frank Potter's behind it all?" asked Crile.

"That's right."

"He's hated me for a long while but I didn't believe he'd kill others because of that."

"He hasn't," said Hatfield. "Potter's a practical hombre. He's after somethin'

141

mightly valuable. I need to check a bit more on his records, then I'll have it clear. He's behind the disappearances of the men from the east bank of the river, and behind the war bein' fomented between the Mace and such decent folks as Mike Brophy. Potter cleverly got rid of east bank folks whose land he wanted and at the same time laid it to the Mace in his plan to wipe you out. I figger he'll push Brophy over the edge, for he needs fightin' men with real nerve to deal with you. Hired guns won't do."

"What do yuh wish me to do?" the colonel asked.

"Pull in yore riders and stay close to home today. If Potter acts like I believe he will, he'll bust wide open when he hears what's happened. Hustle back to yore ranch for the time bein'."

"And you? Aren't you comin' with us?"

"I'm headin' for Mullen City. I got to get hold of Mike Brophy before Potter gets rollin'. I have some ideas I wish yuh'd carry out. Rest yore men today and be ready when I need yuh."

Hatfield gave Madison Crile precise instructions. Then the big Ranger turned the golden sorrel and cantered toward the river. A wave of his long hand was answered by his firm friends of the Mace.

The sun was in his face. He pulled down the Stetson brim. The dust kicked up under the sorrel's shod hoofs as the Ranger called on his reserves of strength. He had rested at the bandit eyrie and he could ride long periods without a letup. The moment for such exertion had come.

The sun rose higher, beating fiercely on horse and rider. The Mace outfit had dropped out of sight, headed for the home ranch.

But Hatfield knew a great part of his task lay before him. He must check the bloody warfare about to smash the range.

Hatfield made a fast run for Mullen City. After a time he could see smoke staining the clear air, smoke from chimneys in the settlement. As he pushed up the stream bank toward the city ford he sighted horsemen galloping for the river. Behind them rose whorls of dust.

"Cuss it. Tate's made it ahead of me!" he thought.

Even had he beaten Tate in this race, however, he was sure that the outlaws at the hideout would have sent a message to let Joe the Knife and Potter know that Lucia Crile had been snatched away from them. He was wary as he neared the west bank of the stream, with the town looming on the other side and up the way a few hundred yards.

A rifle bullet shrieked over him, humming like a giant hornet. Riders appeared as they spurted down the east bank to get a better shot at him.

"Potter's on watch for us, Goldy," he murmured.

The city teemed with his enemies and those who supposed him their antagonist. George Loese, and other Potter agents, as well as the decent element led by Mike Brophy would all be gunning for him. He would be filled with lead before he could locate Brophy and make himself heard.

Slugs hunted him, and they were getting closer. Spurts of dirt jumped up around the moving sorrel, and Hatfield pulled his reins and pivoted to move away. Riders drove their horses into the river as they started across to chase him.

He was certainly on the dodge for he could not draw near enough to make himself known as a Ranger and explain the complicated matter. Loese and others like him would shoot him in the back.

He thought he recognized Frank Potter's big figure in the crowd around the courthouse. Potter would be urging men on while tempers were hot.

Men on dripping mustangs were coming up the west bank after him as he beat a hasty retreat before the blindly firing guns. It was impossible to distinguish between those who might be his friends if they knew who he was, and those who would wish to kill him on sight.

Horsemen fanned out and cut him off from three sides. He was driven gradually west. The golden sorrel had to run at full speed as the ravening pursuers whooped it up and fired on his trail.

CHAPTER XIII
NIGHT RIDE

Night had fallen over the great Mace and Hatfield was waiting for the chunk of moon to come up. It would offer only a faint light and the shadows would be black, but he needed just that.

He had outrun the Mullen City men, and Goldy had had to have rest, after the fast race from the outlaw depot, and the chase after that. Hatfield had gone into bivouac in one of the isolated groves which cut Crile's range. For the time being Potter had checked the Ranger. It was impossible to get into Mullen City in the daytime and any Mace rider who attempted to go through would meet the same fate the plotters against the Mace had tried to mete out to the Ranger.

So he had accepted the situation. When the pursuers had quit after seeing how fast the sorrel was, he had let them drop out of sight, then doubled slowly back until he figured he was near the line of march that an army from Mullen City would take on its way to attack Crile's ranch. He had unsaddled and napped during the hot afternoon, aware that a rested body and mind would serve better than weary ones.

Saddling Goldy, and checking his guns, the Ranger mounted and rode east. He was certain that Frank Potter would strike at once, and in order to surprise the Mace, Potter would try to make his approach at night. And if the counselor failed to hit immediately, then Hatfield hoped to get into Mullen City and reach Mike Brophy.

But he got no such opportunity. An hour later he heard them coming, the shaking of the earth under hundreds of hoofs. He cut south and pulled up in a dark spot where a clump of cottonwoods grew from a rocky path.

"Quiet now, Goldy," he whispered.

He saw the dark riders, but could not make out features for not only was the light poor but they had drawn up their bandannas against dust and perhaps because they were on such a violent mission. Two leaders came first, horses at a slow trot. Behind them came a group of six, then the large main body.

"Must be a couple hundred of 'em!" he

thought.

There would be few known outlaws in this party, made up of ranchers and their cowboys and townsmen of Mullen City, bent on crushing their supposed enemy, the Mace. Loese might be with them, and other agents of Potter's. Perhaps the counselor himself was along.

Certainly Mike Brophy would be there. But in the rising dust, and confusion of the march, Hatfield was unable to identify the rancher. A haze rose from under the many hoofs.

"Got to locate Brophy," decided the Ranger.

He pulled his bandanna up to his eyes and waited until most of them had gone past the grove. A few stragglers could be heard coming along. Hatfield eased the golden sorrel out of the trees and joined the procession without anyone noticing the addition.

Slumped in his saddle the Ranger rode as a sleeper in the army of citizens come to deal a death blow to Crile's Mace.

For half a mile the Ranger carefully worked his way nearer the head of the band. There was not much talk. The men rode in grim silence with ready guns, staring through the risen dust in the pale moonlight.

Hatfield was near the leaders when they stopped. The fighters from Mullen City closed up and the slower ones caught up with the main body.

"All right, boys. We ain't runnin' into any traps." One of the chiefs had turned to address them. It was Mike Brophy, the rancher. "I'm goin' on ahead and check up," continued Brophy. "Crile's a crafty devil and the old cuss may have mounted sentries way out from the buildin's. Mebbe he even has outside defenses and we don't want to stumble into an ambush.

"Counselor Potter will fetch yuh along slow, and yuh'll wait till yuh hear from me. Yuh elected me captain of this band and yuh'll do like I tell yuh. There's a patch of woods up the creek from the Mace that will make a good hidin' place till we're ready for the attack. I'll see yuh there around dawn."

A large figure not far from Brophy was Frank Potter and close at hand, shivering in excitement, was a small rider. Hatfield was sure it was Loese, the jackal, never far from his powerful master.

Brophy rode off in the direction of the Mace. Like a good general he intended making sure of what he was leading his forces against.

The men were rolling smokes and lighting

up as they chatted in low tones.

"Come on, boys," ordered Potter. "We'll make the woods before dawn." He moved away toward the southwest to strike the bank of the stream which fed through the Mace.

Hatfield dropped back and in the dusty night had no difficulty in deserting the procession. He headed on Mike Brophy's trail, sure that the rancher would ride directly toward the Mace. Brophy had had but a few minutes' start.

Picking up speed, Hatfield flashed across the rolling range. Sniffing at the clean air he caught the dust of Brophy's trail and rode on at full-tilt.

He cantered the golden sorrel up a long, gentle incline and on the crest, against the moon, saw a horseman framed. He knew it must be Brophy, and that the rancher had heard him coming. As Hatfield drew in, the faint sheen of the light caught moving metal, the barrel of Brophy's carbine.

"Who's that?" demanded Brophy, leveling his weapon.

"I got a message, Mike!" called the Ranger.

Brophy was an honest citizen and there was little danger in approaching the man. He waited and peered at the tall rider, trying to see who it was.

"Potter send yuh?" he asked, as Hatfield pulled up short and danced Goldy around so he could talk.

"I'm here on account of Potter," replied the Ranger. "My handle is Jim Hatfield and I'm a Texas Ranger from Austin."

Brophy jumped in his leather, and cursed. "A Ranger! Why didn't yuh come before? I warn yuh, don't interfere now. We're carryin' out our own justice."

Brophy was upset, but he was a strong character, as Hatfield had judged, and not easily deflected once his mind was made up.

"I wouldn't blame yuh for hittin' the Mace if things were as they have been made to look," said the Ranger levelly. "Texas is a mighty big place, and sometimes the decent folks have to take the law into their own hands to protect themselves."

Brophy was angry at first, then puzzled, and later interested as he listened to the big officer. Briefly, but fully, the Ranger outlined to him the entire situation.

When Hatfield said quietly, "If yuh'll come along, Brophy, I'll show yuh the body of yore brother," the rancher agreed. He studied Hatfield's credentials by the light of a flaring match and then the two men rode back northward together.

An hour later, not far from the spur which projected down from the hills, Hatfield ordered, "Wait here, Brophy." He moved toward the black grove south of the diminishing spine of rock and called softly:

"Colonel Crile!"

Madison Crile was there, according to Hatfield's orders. He had several riders with him, Mace fighting men. Crile came out to join the big Ranger.

"Leave yore boys here for a jiffy till we talk with Brophy," said Hatfield.

Brophy swore as he came face to face with Colonel Crile. He would not shake hands, and held himself stiffly.

"Yore men killed my brother, Crile," he growled.

"Potter and his outlaws killed him," said Hatfield gravely. "We'll prove it to yuh, Brophy. It means a long ride, but I'll guarantee to convince yuh."

"I ain't ridin' with Crile," snapped Brophy.

Crile suppressed his flaring temper and pride. "We used to be friends, Brophy," he said calmly. "I believe what Ranger Hatfield says. I know it's true. Otherwise I wouldn't be here, with my loved ones in danger at the ranch."

Jeff Crile and Corky Ellsworth were in command at the Mace ranchhouse, and Crile himself had obeyed Hatfield's request to wait at this designated point. It had taken the utmost faith in Hatfield to make Madison Crile leave home at such a perilous moment.

The magic of the Ranger prevailed over Brophy but the blunt rancher from Mullen City was hard to change, for he had been tricked by Potter into charging all evil to the Mace. But Brophy finally rode with Hatfield and Crile, trailed by the half-dozen Mace fighters.

Hatfield hit the trail toward the outlaw stronghold and they forged ahead at the fastest possible pace. . . .

It was not far from dawn when the Ranger crept forward afoot to check on the bandit hideout. As he had thought, there were only a few in the basin. Joe the Knife and the main bunch of gunslingers were somewhere on the range, probably awaiting Potter's orders.

Hatfield returned to Crile and Brophy. Mike Brophy sat his horse in grim silence apart from the Mace riders, whom he still blamed for the death of his younger brother.

"We'll rush the guard," said the Ranger.

"There ain't many in there."

They dismounted and, with drawn guns, moved quietly along the beaten trail. Hatfield knew the spot where the sentry was posted and suddenly the challenge came. The Ranger's Colt flared. The guard answered and it marked his exact position near the big tree. Several pistols spoke and the sentry yelped. There was a crashing in the bushes as the wounded outlaw fell.

"Follow me!" cried Hatfield, and rushed over the rim.

Harry Tate was in command at the stronghold. The shots and yells had awakened the outlaws and they were rolling from their blankets and snatching up guns. Hatfield went down the rocky steps and ran over the uneven ground. The sallow Tate was standing in the faint glow of the fire, pulling a pistol from his holster.

"Throw down, Tate!" cried the Ranger.

The officer was several paces ahead of Crile and Brophy. Tate swore as he raised his Colt, not heeding the order hurled at him by the charging Hatfield. The Ranger lifted his thumb from the hammer spur of his revolver and the gun roared.

Tate was knocked around and fell to one knee. His arm dropped and he rolled on his side. Volleys came from Brophy and the

Crile faction.

There were only a few other gunslingers at the hideout, and they were trapped against the steep rock walls. With everything against them, they began tossing away their arms and begging for mercy. Hatfield and the Mace cowboys quickly secured them.

A gray streak showed in the eastern sky. The world was beginning to lighten as the tall Ranger led Brophy and Crile down the path behind the outlaw eyrie and on through the woods until they came to the cut.

Here he showed Brophy the grave of his brother and opened it.

"It's Ed, no doubt of it," said Brophy sadly. He fought against his emotion.

"I'm mighty sorry, Brophy," Colonel Crile said softly. "The Mace had nothin' to do with this or any of the other missin' men."

"They're all buried around here," explained Hatfield. "Potter planned it all, with the aid of his outlaw allies. He wanted to wreck the Mace and destroy the Criles, Brophy. Rob Davis, yore brother Ed, and the rest were spirited away at night by Potter and his killers, shot down and fetched here. It roused the whole country against Crile. Do yuh believe me now, Mike?"

"I believe yuh," Brophy nodded. He turned to Madison Crile and held out his hand. "Will yuh shake, Crile? We were fooled, and I'm sorry."

Colonel Crile seized Brophy's extended hand. "I understand. The Mace was deceived too, by a mighty clever rascal. Frank Potter."

Crile was jumpy because he knew that far south Potter commanded the citizen army plus Joe the Knife's outlaws. They might wait for a time for Mike Brophy to return but when he did not appear within a reasonable time Potter would no doubt prevail and push them in against the Mace. The colonel feared for his loved ones and friends.

"Let's ride!" ordered the Ranger, as much aware of the danger as was Crile.

"I'll tell yuh more of the setup as we move."

Two Mace *vaqueros* were left to guard the prisoners at the hideout. The others followed Hatfield, Brophy and Crile as they headed for the great ranch to deal with Potter.

Hatfield regretted the lost hours, but it had been vital to convince Mike Brophy and bring the chief of the Mullen City contingent over to the right side.

"I want to come up behind that woods on the creek just north of yore ranch, Crile," explained the Ranger. "That's where Potter is s'posed to hold the attackers."

"Then we better ride down the west bank," replied the colonel. "We'll have more cover to approach behind."

CHAPTER XIV
BATTLE

Potter might even now be hitting Crile's home, so the Colonel was tense. Brophy, saddened by the proof of his brother's death, rode along with his chin down and a grim set to his strong face.

The sun was up when they sighted the woods before them, across the winding stream which was fringed with growth and offered them concealment. They crossed the little creek and entered the trees but as Brophy forged ahead, to find his friends, there was no large collection of Mullen City fighters to be seen.

Brophy waited for them on the east side of the patch.

"They're gone," he growled.

Hatfield strained his ears. The breeze was intermittent from the south and on it he caught faint explosions.

"Potter's attackin'!" he said. "Let's go! We've got to stop it before it's too late!"

They rode at full speed for the Mace home spread and as they neared the great ranch, the crackling of many guns grew more and more audible. Reaching a crest the Ranger saw the buildings before him, saw Mullen City men dismounted and lying behind rocks or other slight protection offered by the terrain.

They were shooting at the windows, and from the house came answering shots. The mass attempt to smash the Mace had begun!

Madison Crile was like a madman as he saw his home under siege.

"Hurry!" begged the colonel, his agitation pitiful.

"You lie well back till I signal yuh," ordered the Ranger. "It's vital. They'll fire on yuh at sight. We got to give Brophy a chance to talk to 'em. C'mon, Mike! It's up to you now!"

Hatfield realized that he was in as much danger of being shot down by the excited fighters in the heat of the battle as Colonel Crile was, but he did not hesitate. Potter and his agents had wrecked the Ranger's standing in Mullen City, and good men as well as evil ones were gunning for the tall rider on the golden sorrel. The officer was depending on Mike Brophy to call off the attack on the Mace, gather the citizens

159

together and make them listen to the truth about the situation.

For this Hatfield had spent precious hours, and he had risked his life to prove the truth of his accusations to Mike Brophy, the chosen leader of the better elements. He had run Brophy through to the outlaw depot and shown him the remains of the men missing from Mullen City, among them those of Ed Brophy, Mike's younger brother. But always on a complicated, perilous case Ranger Jim Hatfield enlisted the honest men of a community, once he had determined the right and wrong of a matter. Just as he was depending on Brophy now. He knew that Mike Brophy would be safe among his friends but there was no safety for Colonel Crile. The Colonel knew that also and, as eager as he was to reach his home, he obeyed Hatfield's order and hung back.

"I'm worried," said Brophy, glancing at the Ranger.

"How so, Mike?" asked Hatfield.

"Potter said somethin' about fetchin' along bombs to blast holes in the *hacienda* walls. He may have a couple tossed in there any minute!"

"Hustle then! Get in there! Call off yore friends and tell 'em the truth. I'll speak to 'em when yuh have 'em in the mood to listen."

Brophy spurred forward, shouting and gesticulating to attract the attention of his comrades. Hatfield followed slowly, the silver star on silver circle glinting in the sun.

"There's Potter over on the far side," muttered Hatfield. "No danger of a stray slug nippin' his precious hide in the shelter of them rocks!"

East of the buildings a red shale outcrop offered excellent protection, and Potter had taken advantage of it. He seemed to be directing the battle from this point. The small figure of George Loese, Potter's jackal, bobbed near his chief, but in general Loese kept crouched down. He made no attempt to join the fight.

Hatfield drew the carbine from under his leg and cocked it. He had noted that Potter had several metal containers beside him and while it was difficult to determine just what the counselor was up to at such a distance, with the sun in the Ranger's eyes, Hatfield thought that Potter might be making ready explosives to breach the thick walls of the *hacienda*.

In the house Jeff Crile, Corky Ellsworth and other Mace fighters had manned the openings to defend the main structure. Bullets smacked into the adobe, sprays of brick and metal fragments flying from the spots where they hit. Better aimed bullets ripped through windows into the interior of the ranchhouse.

There were several men behind the rocks with Frank Potter, and four saddled mustangs stood nearby with dropped reins, though most of the horses which had brought the east bank army to the Mace had been left well back out of range of stray lead. Hatfield could see that Potter was giving the fighters near him careful orders. Each accepted a canister from Potter.

"There go the bombs!" thought the Ranger. "Wonder how close I could come to that cuss Potter?"

He raised his carbine and took careful aim. He squeezed trigger, and Frank Potter jumped and quickly dropped to a crouch, getting well out of sight close to the red outcrop. Loese was terrified by the hum of death, and groveled flat on the ground, pushing in against a boulder.

A horseman came around the rocks behind Potter. He was carrying one of the canisters, fused and ready to light and throw in at the adobe walls of the *hacienda*. He was a cowboy from one of the small ranches on the east bank, a misguided enthusiast whipped to killing hate against the Mace by Potter's manipulations. He was risking his life to dash in and toss the explosives.

Hatfield had no desire to kill such a man. He threw another shell into his carbine and, taking a bead on the cowboy's mount, squeezed his trigger again. He thought he had missed but the mustang slowed after a few steps. The cowboy jumped off, running, and the horse collapsed.

The Ranger looked to see how Mike Brophy was doing. The stocky rancher had succeeded in calling around him a dozen of his friends — ranchers, cowboys and Mullen City men. Brophy was talking fast as he explained what he had learned through the Ranger.

Quickly the aides Brophy had collected hurried from their leader and fanned out, yelling orders to their companions to cease firing. The guns slackened until only a few from the far side kept speaking.

The sun caught something at the rock outcrop where Potter was hiding. The light touched field-glasses which Frank Potter had trained on the tall rider on the sorrel, then swept around to cover Brophy. Potter ducked back as if panic-stricken.

"There he goes!" murmured Hatfield.

Potter suddenly came into his range of vision again, but now he was on a big black gelding and picking up speed as he headed for the river and Mullen City. Potter had recognized that Ranger star, and guessed what must have occurred, and somehow Brophy had been apprised of the truth. And Potter was too shrewd an operator to be caught easily.

In a few moments George Loese flogged out on a gray mustang, following his master.

The Ranger tried for both Potter and Loese, but his shots went wide.

More and more men were gathering around Mike Brophy now and finally as Hatfield moved the sorrel in, Brophy signaled the Ranger.

Colonel Madison Crile came slowly over the crest and approached the gathering, of his erstwhile enemies.

"Hold everything boys!" bawled Mike Brophy, a blunt hand raised. "We've made a big mistake! Frank Potter and Loese, along with the bunch of outlaws led by Joe the Knife and Harry Tate, have throwed dust in our eyes. Here's Ranger Jim Hatfield, who came to settle our trouble. Let him tell yuh all about it!"

Hatfield pulled up beside Brophy and raised a slim hand in salute. The chinstrap of the Ranger's Stetson was taut under his rugged jaw and there was a cold light darkening his gray-green eyes. Power exuded from him, the physical fighting strength of a supple panther and the mental strength to match it as these men saw him in his true might.

The Ranger turned to beckon Madison Crile to join the silenced forces. Jeff Crile and Ellsworth stopped their men shooting, for those defending the *hacienda* could see that Colonel Crile and the Ranger had arrived.

A couple of armed Mullen City fighters came trotting up from the far side of the battlefield. They had not yet heard the truth and, seeing Colonel Crile, their hatred for the Mace chief welled up.

"Why, there's that cuss of a Crile!" bellowed one, a big, bearded townsman.

He threw up his rifle, but Mike Brophy pushed his horse between Crile and the gun muzzle.

"Drop it, Terry!" snapped Brophy. "There's been a mistake."

Dust showed where Frank Potter and George Loese spurred and flogged their horses as they sought to put distance between themselves and the Ranger and those they had tricked into such awful conflict.

Then Hatfield spoke briefly to the assembled men.

"Boys, yuh've been bamboozled by a mighty clever operator, Frank Potter, into fightin' the Mace. No honest hombre has ever been shot by Crile's riders. A passel of outlaws have been hidin' in Crile's hills to the northwest. They carried off certain townsmen and ranchers from the east bank, killed 'em, and hid the bodies. Now Brophy knows it. His brother Ed was one of the victims.

"Potter had a good reason for all he's done. It wasn't only that he hates Colonel Crile, who saw Potter turn tail and run in the war, but Potter has been after somethin' mighty valuable that he hoped to win by puttin' key figgers out of his way. I got a good idea of what Potter wanted, but I need to check up a little more on his office files. There's some letters there will tell what we have to know to fill in the blanks.

"Put up yore guns, and shake hands with the Mace outfit. They're yore friends. Yore real enemies are Potter, Loese, Joe the Knife, and his band."

Mike Brophy held out his hand to Madison Crile and the two men solemnly engaged in a handshake.

Hatfield was eager to be on Potter's trail. He was aware that the counselor was the arch source of all the evil which had come upon the range. And he also must run down Joe the Knife, the bony outlaw boss who had killed a young Texas Ranger and lived to boast about it. But he restrained his impatience as Colonel Crile, at Brophy's side, addressed the gathering:

"I'm mighty sorry about the misunderstandin' and all the trouble. Every decent citizen is my friend and welcome on Mace range at any time. All we've done has been in self-defense, and the Mace was fooled as well as you folks. I expect to open my doors in a few minutes, and I hope yuh'll all be my guests."

Hatfield nudged Mike Brophy. "I'm goin' after Potter. He's headed for the tall timber."

"I'll go with yuh," Brophy said promptly.

"I'm ridin' fast," warned the Ranger. "And it may not be so easy if I run into Joe the Knife's bunch."

He moved away, and picked up speed as he took up the trail of risen dust which marked Potter's retreat.

CHAPTER XV
DUEL

Settled down to the chase, the golden sorrel seemed to fly. The great Mace range opened out once he had reached the rise from the shallow, wide valley of the stream on which stood the home ranch. In the distance could be seen bunches of Mace steers, for the gunfire had alarmed the cattle and caused them to move off.

For a half-hour the grim Ranger kept on at full speed — which was something at which to marvel. For Goldy could outrun anything on four legs and Hatfield was a master horseman. Hatfield knew where he was going, too. That line of dust settling slowly back in the warm air showed that Potter was headed for Mullen City.

"I reckon he's got to pick up money and other things at his office, before he runs for it," thought the Ranger.

He reached a final crest in the wave-like formation of the earth and in the rising dust

168

saw George Loese, a poor second to Counselor Potter, goading his mustang with cruel spurs and beating the bleeding haunches of his horse with his quirt.

There was reason for Loese's terror, for the small man, glancing back over his shoulder had seen the big Ranger coming. Loese knew Hatfield's speed with guns and he now realized exactly who and what the tall fighting man was. The sight of Hatfield sent Loese into a fresh panic and the little man, who had done the undercover work for the powerful Potter, dug in his rowels.

When Hatfield had come up within a dozen yards, Loese turned and fired at the Ranger, but Loese's hand shook and the pace was jolting. The bullets went far wide of their mark. Loese flung the empty gun away and huddled over his saddle.

With a final spurt Hatfield drove up and, reaching out a long arm, caught Loese by the collar. A knee touch sent Goldy veering to the left. Loese came loose from his leather seat and hung for a moment in the air. He was trying to shriek for mercy but fright clogged his throat. His eyes were round with terror.

Hatfield let go and Loese rolled over and over on the ground and lay still, his head against a stone.

Not far ahead, the Ranger sighted Frank Potter, beating his fast black on toward Mullen City. A grove of cottonwoods and brush rose a short distance ahead and Porter seemed to be swinging to put this between himself and his Nemesis.

Hatfield saw Potter turn, throw a short-barreled carbine to his shoulder and pull trigger. The Ranger held his own fire, waiting until he could be sure of reaching Potter.

Potter was shouting and waving. Hatfield stared at the little patch of woods, an island in the range. And the next minute, from the grove, rode a line of horsemen, placing themselves between the Ranger and his prey.

There were thirty of them, and they were led by the bony outlaw, Joe the Knife!

The Knife rode a fast mustard-colored horse. He was a fine rider and handled his mount as well as any man Hatfield had ever seen. The steeple sombrero he sported was canted at a rakish angle on the tall bandit's narrow head. The white knife scar stood out on his left cheek. The killer carried not only his pistols and his knife, but a carbine which he raised and fired as he rode on toward the Ranger.

In the open, Hatfield would die if they came up with him. He might take several along but it was sure death to face such a force.

Frank Potter kept going. His outlaw allies had thrown themselves between him and the law.

With Joe the Knife, were the bandits with whom Hatfield had consorted at the hideout. He knew them all, knew how tough they could be when they had the upper hand. They would fill him with lead once they caught him. Reluctantly Hatfield pulled his reins, turning the sorrel and retreating before the onslaught of the outlaw line.

Joe the Knife was whooping it up as he called on his men to overtake the Ranger. On the mustard-hued horse the Knife drew out in front of his hellions.

They came after Hatfield pell-mell, passing the small figure of George Loese which lay on the plain unnoticed. Either Loese was knocked out or fright had paralyzed his muscles, for he did not move as the running scrap tore past him.

Hatfield was driven before the fury of the outlaws. He headed back toward the Mace, for he was sure that Mike Brophy would be along with a contingent of fighting men who could deal with Joe the Knife's band.

"Wonder what Potter said to the Knife

that makes him so foolhardy?" thought the Ranger.

He was surprised that the outlaws would be so bold as to ride into the face of such danger. Potter must have lied to them whole-heartedly in order to give himself a chance to escape. It would delay the pursuit of the counselor for the avengers to have to deal with Joe the Knife.

"Reckon he told 'em everything was under control except me," he muttered.

They came on, closer and closer to the Mace and to whatever force Brophy might be bringing up to support the Ranger. Joe the Knife, on his superior mount and riding with the greatest skill, was two hundred yards ahead of his main band as Hatfield again glanced back to check on the situation.

"Yuh s'pose the Knife would fall for that old trick, Goldy?" muttered the Ranger to the galloping sorrel.

He slowed a bit, allowing Joe the Knife to gain a few more paces. Seeing he was catching his tall foe, the Knife redoubled his efforts and yelled in triumph, gun cocked and ready in his hand. Hatfield held his fire and so did the Knife. The distance between them shortened, as the two powerful horses tore along.

Joe the Knife, killer of a Texas Ranger, drew nearer and nearer. Hatfield swerved and the sorrel ran south, then came around as the Ranger deliberately brought his horse about so that he was facing his enemy.

The Knife recognized that silver star on silver circle. He knew then that Hatfield wanted him in particular, and suddenly he realized what he had run into. He pulled hard on his reins and glanced quickly back to see if his men were coming, but they were vital seconds away.

"Yuh've killed yore last Ranger, Joe!" called Hatfield.

Fate stared the Knife in his deep-set eyes. His fierce face worked with anger and the white scar on his cheek twisted with his writhing lips. He sought to bring his gun around for a kill.

Hatfield used his heavy carbine. The sorrel steadied for the shot and Hatfield's eye was clear, his touch unshaken and expert. The bullet ripped from the muzzle and Joe the Knife caught it in the nose. It ranged up into his brain and the killer sagged as his rifle exploded too late.

The outlaws following him yipped as they saw Joe the Knife falling from saddle. The mustard gelding had shied from the blasts and the twist threw the Knife off. The mustang trotted on for a short distance and Joe the Knife was dragged in the dust, a long-booted foot caught in the tapped stirrup.

"Ain't got the time to check on him, but he shore looks dead," growled Hatfield.

It was growing too hot there for the Ranger as Joe's infuriated followers tried to avenge the death of their leader.

Hatfield pulled the sorrel around and picked up speed. He looked back to see the Knife lying still, while the outlaw chief's horse calmly put down his muzzle to graze. The bandits swept on past Joe the Knife, two dropping out to see if there was anything they could do for the dead chief.

The Ranger rode on, gaining on the foe. Dust rose before him in the direction of the Mace, and he was sure it marked the band led by Mike Brophy, hurrying to offer the Ranger their assistance.

"Mebbe we can sweep up the whole bunch of outlaws, Goldy!" he muttered, gauging the chance.

He led them on, keeping just out of easy gun range. Now he was certain that Potter had lied to the bandits to give himself time to run, or they would never have ventured so close to the Mace.

Then horrified outlaw eyes sighted the big

174

contingent of fighting men coming toward them at a smart clip. Hatfield laughed, for he could imagine their feelings at seeing Mike Brophy and Colonel Crile riding together at the head of Mace *vaqueros* and east bank men.

It told everything, and the bandits pulled up in clouds of dust, whirled and pelted off in every direction.

Mike Brophy and Colonel Crile shouted and waved to the Ranger who pointed at the running outlaws. Bunches of avenging Mace riders and east bank men split off to rush hard and sweep up the gunslingers who had haunted the range.

There was no cover for the stricken killers, and one by one they were run down. The death of their bony chief, Joe the Knife, had disheartened them and few chose to fight to the death. Instead, they threw away their guns and raised their hands in surrender. Crile's men and the men from Mullen City and the ranches east of the line quickly took their prisoners. Only three of Joe the Knife's powerful band managed to escape on fast mustangs which carried them swirling away in clouds of dust.

"That dust is the last we'll see of those cusses," remarked the Ranger.

He fixed a quirly and relaxed, a long leg cocked against his saddle-horn.

CHAPTER XVI
RECORD

Loese had been brought in by Mace riders. They had found the little spy playing dead on the flat where he had been hurled when the Ranger had caught him.

Under the stern eyes of those he had helped to wrong, George Loese trembled and whimpered. Colonel Crile scowled at the captive and Mike Brophy was angry, too, at having been stampeded into such a mistaken position by the machinations of Potter and this little crook.

"Yuh'll pay for this, Loese," threatened Brophy.

"Yuh've done a great deal of harm," added Crile.

"I — it ain't my fault," whined Loese, shaking so that his teeth chattered. "Potter made me do it."

"Hold him," ordered the Ranger. "He'll do to fill in the blanks for us if we need 'em filled, gents. Yuh'll sing a song for me, won't yuh, George?"

"Yes, anything," promised Loese. "Only just don't let 'em kill me!"

They were all contemptuous of the cowardly spy. Rough hands secured Loese.

"How about Frank Potter?" inquired Madison Crile, his bearded face stern.

"I ain't forgot him," drawled Jim Hatfield. "Just been givin' my hoss a breather. Then I was goin' after him. I figger he'll head for that office of his in Mullen City. He must have money and other things he'll want to pick up. He threw Joe the Knife and his bunch to the wolves when the goin' got hard, to save his own precious hide."

"That's Potter all over," Crile answered.

"I'm startin' after him," said Hatfield. "Colonel, will yuh come along with a few riders, and I'd like to talk to you, too, Mike. Fetch Loese with yuh to town. Yore boys can handle these outlaw prisoners and lock 'em up in the city jail. I don't reckon Potter will be around Mullen City to defend 'em this time."

Brophy and Crile smiled. They gave commands to their men as the tall officer on the golden sorrel saluted and, throwing away his smoke, started on Frank A. Potter's trail. . . .

Mullen City baked under the hot sun of

the Southwest. The settlement seemed to be deserted. Most of the able-bodied men had ridden with Mike Brophy and Potter against the Mace and the women and older folks were keeping inside out of the sun.

Hatfield had ridden straight for the town, guessing that Potter would chance a flying stop at his home before he set out for other parts.

"I hope he don't have time to destroy that secret file of his," he thought as he cantered up the dusty street, keeping to the center.

The keen gray-green eyes hunted the corners and other possible spots where Potter might lurk if the lawyer should try to pick him off on his way into town, but he saw no sign of the man.

The Ranger drew up and tossed Goldy's reins over the rail a few doors down from Potter's house. The office door stood open and Hatfield watched it, but still no sign of the lawyer.

"I hope he ain't shortcut and run for it!" thought Hatfield.

That could mean a long chase. Potter might even reach a haven where it would be difficult to arrest him. Hatfield began to fear that his hunch had been wrong.

He moved swiftly along the wooden walk, the loose boards creaking under his booted feet, spurs faintly jingling. Sweat stained his shirt and his leather pants were scratched by thorns. There was a smudge of gun powder on one bronzed cheek and the Stetson strap accented his set jaw. His eyes flicked from spot to spot, and his big Colts gently rubbed in the oiled holsters.

He slowed as he reached Potter's door. Through the opening he saw the flat-topped desk with weighted papers on it. He expected a shot from a window but none came, and he made a quick jump inside.

"He's been here," he thought.

The office was empty. That special drawer had been unlocked and several folders lay strewn on the floor. It looked as though Potter had been disturbed at his work and had dropped everything.

Hatfield glanced at the closed connecting door to the counselor's living quarters. He strode to it and standing to one side, lifted the latch and kicked the door open. The second door was also shut and he negotiated it in the same fashion.

Potter had three large rooms in the rear, a well-furnished living room, a sunny bedroom and a spacious kitchen. A couple of drawers in the bureau stood open and a clean shirt lay on the rug before it.

The Ranger felt a faint draft and, after

making sure that Potter was not hiding under a bed or in the closet, he went through to the back entry. The door stood open and he could look along a gravel path with a yard on either side of the stable and small corral.

Frank Potter had just finished saddling a fresh horse, a handsome gray gelding with a dark spot on his arched neck. The black mustang on which he had escaped from the field of defeat, stood with head down and feet spread, run to a frazzle. Indignation, another tally against Potter, flushed Hatfield, for blood had matted the black's coat where Potter's cruel spurs had raked, and Potter had flogged the animal near death. The black was done for and knew it.

The Ranger rushed from the kitchen door and his boots kicked up gravel on the path as he headed straight at the man. Potter saw him coming and his face twisted in fearful rage.

"Reach, Potter!" roared Hatfield.

But Counselor Potter knew how he stood. He whipped up a six-shooter and fired at the man who had run him into the ground.

Hatfield's Colts were still in the holsters, flapping against his thighs as he ran on. The gray gelding whirled in alarm at the cracking gun so close to him, and shouldered heavily against Potter, wrecking his aim.

The Ranger pulled up short only yards from Potter. His long hand flicked and a pistol flew with blinding speed to his grip. A breath later Hatfield fired, shading Potter's fatal bead.

Potter's third try kicked up gravel. He shuddered as heavy lead ripped into him. He slumped and his arm fell to his side, the revolver dropping from his relaxing fingers. His knees seemed turned to rubber as he crumpled.

The Ranger strode on to stand over him. Potter was still breathing, but in awful gasps. Blood pumped from a wound under his heart. The man was dying and knew it, as the grim officer waited.

Colonel Crile, Mike Brophy and their men, Mace riders and ranchers as well as citizens of Mullen City, grouped in the defunct Potter's office, listening to the big Ranger as he explained to them the machinations of the counselor.

"Potter was after a big stake, gents," said Jim Hatfield, as he sat on the edge of the desk facing them all. "He wanted the Mace and he wanted key lands belongin' to east bank men. I've gone over his records and correspondence and Loese has talked and told me my ideas were just about right. It's like this. Up in the northwest sections of the Mace lie big deposits of sphalerite and calamine. These are worth a fortune."

"What's that?" asked Brophy.

"They're ores of the metal zinc," explained Hatfield. "I run onto an outcrop behind Joe the Knife's hideout, where the missin' hombres were buried. Potter discovered the stuff through the outlaws who hid in the hills. He went to a lot of trouble having the samples analyzed.

"I found reports from city chemists and letters from a big manufacturer, the Z-N Company, sayin' that if the ore deposits come up to specifications, they would be worth plenty. Potter worked it all out. He hated Crile and he was glad to figger a way to wreck the Mace so that he could seize it. With the Criles out of the runnin' he knew he could get the ranch and so own the zinc ores."

"Why did he kill Rob Davis and my brother and the rest?" asked Mike Brophy.

"It fitted in with his plan to finish off the Criles," replied the Ranger. "The mysterious disappearance of yore friends could be laid to the Mace, while Joe the Knife and his outlaws kept Crile ruffled up so the colonel thought he was bein' put upon as well.

Killin' two birds with one stone, so to speak, Potter was takin' over properties around Mullen City. He had either forged deeds and ousted the rightful heir, or he would get an option for a small amount down.

"Yuh see, these zinc compounds are used in platin', makin' paints, medicines and other important products. But it takes smelterin' and chemicals to get 'em separated from the iron and other impurities, so a plant was needed and the Z-N firm intended to build in Mullen City. That meant a railroad through the town and a spur up to the mines. Potter was in line of bein' king of the whole shebang once he got rid of the Criles and a few others."

Crile and the east bank men heard the Ranger's explanation of Potter's machinations. There was restoration to be made to the victims who still lived, and the tall officer made sure that all would be taken care of.

Captain Bill McDowell stamped an impatient foot as he looked from his south window for the hundredth time that afternoon.

"He ought to be showin'," he growled. "His telegram said he'd be in before this."

Then he sighted the tall rider coming on

the golden sorrel and he relaxed, going to the door to wait as Hatfield rode into the yard at Austin headquarters and took care of the handsome gelding.

Inside, when Hatfield came in, McDowell sat in his chair and listened to his star operative's terse report. He knew Hatfield, and could fill in between the short lines.

"Hombre named Potter, the lawyer who defended Joe the Knife, was workin' a cute game down there, rilin' the folks against the Mace," explained Hatfield. "He won't do any more of it, Cap'n Bill. And Joe the Knife won't shoot any more Rangers."

"Fine, fine."

McDowell skillfully probed for the story.

"So this young Corky Ellsworth is marryin' Crile's daughter and he's with the Mace. And I reckon the zinc ores will make those people down there right well-off."

The Ranger nodded. He had spruced up on his way back to report and looked fresh and calm. McDowell considered him.

"Yore hoss don't seem too wore out, either," he observed.

"No, suh. We took it easy on the road back. Had some hard ridin' for a while around the Mace."

The old captain picked up a report and rattled it. He cleared his throat and frowned

185

as he stared at the written complaints.

"Yuh're entitled to a vacation, Hatfield. I wouldn't blame yuh if yuh took it."

A smile touched the wide mouth. Hatfield knew his captain. He knew that McDowell had only a handful of officers with which to patrol and control huge Texas. In the southeast brush country, on the vast central range, along the Red River hundreds of miles west over the Staked Plain, on the Rio Grande and the Gulf Coast, and across the Pecos where there was said to be no law at all, outlaws hid themselves and sallied forth on evil missions. The Rangers must defeat such bands.

"What yuh got?" demanded Hatfield. "I'll take it."

"It's a big job," warned McDowell. "Otherwise I wouldn't bother yuh. It's a new wrinkle some hombre who thinks he's clever is puttin' across on folks near the Edwards Plateau where it edges the Pecos."

Hatfield listened to the complaints and checked up on what information was available.

Not long after, McDowell stood in the yard at headquarters, watching the tall officer on the golden sorrel as Jim Hatfield rode off westward, again carrying Ranger law to the land.

CPSIA information can be obtained at www.ICGtesting.com
Printed in the USA
LVOW04n0428110813

347154LV00001B/1/P